The Author

While she was still in her teens, Barbara C. Freeman had to decide between a career as an artist or as a writer. She chose art and spent the next three years at the Kingston School of Art in her native England. Her first job after graduation was as a copyist with a London firm that specialized in exact, hand-painted reproductions of old Chinese wallpapers. She gave this up after a year to become a free-lance illustrator of children's books.

Miss Freeman especially likes such subjects as traditional fairy tales in which historical costume can be used, and she maintains her own reference collection for this purpose. She began to write for children shortly after World War II and soon sold some short stories and rhymes, which she illustrated herself. *Lucinda* is the third of Miss Freeman's books to be published in the United States.

LUCINDA

LUCINDA

written and illustrated

by

BARBARA C. FREEMAN

W • W • NORTON & COMPANY INC • •

NEW YORK

Contents

7

Chapter 1

THIRTEENTH BIRTHDAY:
THE MANOR

December 1856

TODAY, DECEMBER 4TH 1856, IS MY THIRTEENTH BIRTHDAY AND
Mamma gave me, as usual, the painted ivory fan she used
when she was a girl. Since we have no money and cannot buy
presents, Mamma gives the fan to each of us in turn. Flora
receives it on her birthday and returns it in time for Isabella's
birthday and Isabella returns it in time for mine. That has
been the family arrangement ever since we came to Uncle
Pescott's house seven years ago.

As for George and Harry, they share Papa's silver watch.
On birthdays too Mamma gives us a holiday from lessons.

After breakfast Uncle Pescott sent for me to come to the
library. I went unwillingly and yet with a kind of hope,
thinking that perhaps, after all, he had recollected that it was
my birthday. Since Papa died and we were forced to move
from London and live in the country with Uncle Pescott, we
have had so few things we could call our own that even the
smallest present seems extremely precious.

Mamma acts as housekeeper for Uncle Pescott but receives
no salary because we are all given board and lodgings. She
says she is thankful that Uncle Pescott offered us a home be-

9

cause otherwise she would have had to go out as a governess again and our family might have been broken up. But she grows ever paler and more anxious as Uncle Pescott grows more exacting.

Uncle Pescott was a merchant's clerk in London before he unexpectedly inherited the Manor, the Manor Farm, all the fields and woods of Rindle Green and most of the cottages in the village.

I knocked on the library door, entered quietly and said, "Good morning, Uncle Pescott."

Uncle Pescott was sitting behind his great desk and did not immediately look up, so I turned to study the new painting that was leaning against the wall. Uncle Pescott is always buying pictures and other objects for the Manor. I have sometimes thought that it is the only thing in the world that he loves.

I did not like the new painting. It depicted two dogs and a poor dead hare. There was a dark, dreadful sky behind them. "Well?" said Uncle Pescott, in his sudden sharp voice. "What do you think of it?"

"It's very sad," I said.

Uncle Pescott crossed the room and stood behind me. He is a short gentleman, with a narrow face, which usually looks fierce unless he is endeavouring to be amiable. He walks with a curious prancing step.

"It was a great bargain," he said. "Observe the manner in which the highlights are touched in. I flatter myself I know a masterpiece when I see one."

"But you've such a large number of pictures, Uncle Pescott," I said. "I can't imagine where you'll hang it."

"One can always find room," said Uncle Pescott. "I hear that Lord Elliston has a fine collection of old family portraits, but I doubt if even he has a more life-like representation of a hare. I believe I will invite him over one day to examine it."

"Yes," I said and wished Uncle Pescott would tell me why he had sent for me.

He returned to his desk and began to sort his papers, so I moved a little nearer to the fire. We are so seldom warm in our rooms that it was a pleasure to watch the flames curling round the huge logs and twisting up the chimney. The library is always the warmest room in the house.

Uncle Pescott looked up. "That fellow who came from Ramsford to clear the school-room chimney is claiming five shillings and sixpence," he said.

"He worked in the school-room for a long time," I said, "but the chimney still smokes."

"He told me a whole farrago of nonsense," said Uncle Pescott, "and insisted that he would have to break into the chimney to discover what was blocking it. So I sent him away."

"But, Uncle Pescott, the chimney still smokes," I said. "Sometimes when we're at our lessons with Mamma we can scarcely see for smoke."

"These country fellows are all rogues," said Uncle Pescott. "They think, because I came from London, that they can cheat me with impunity. I have to watch them pretty carefully, I can tell you."

"I think you wished to tell me something, Uncle Pescott," I said.

Uncle Pescott picked up a handful of papers and looked at them, frowning. Then he looked at me. "I sent for you," he said, "to make it clear why I am in no position to present you with a gift on your birthday."

As Uncle Pescott has never given any of us a present this remark astonished me.

"You must understand that the expenses of this establishment are exorbitant and grow more overwhelming every day," said Uncle Pescott. "Flora and Isabella are now such great girls and George and Harry have such dreadful appetites that I am sometimes at a loss to know how to keep the household expenses within bounds. Your mother's poor health is a very serious inconvenience to me. If she were a better manager—but I will say no more of that."

I longed to point out to Uncle Pescott that Mamma's terrible headaches were rather more inconvenient to her than to him. But I remained silent.

Whenever any of us annoys Uncle Pescott it is always Mamma who is blamed. Uncle Pescott stood up and began to walk about the room.

"I understand what you've told me, Uncle Pescott," I said. "May I go now?"

"All in good time," said Uncle Pescott. "What I have told you is only the necessary introduction to clear your mind, as it were, of any expectations. But I have something further to announce that will, I believe, cause great satisfaction to you all. And since it is your birthday today, Lucinda, I have selected you to bear the good tidings to your brothers and sisters." He paused, waiting, I suppose, for my thanks, but I said nothing, so he continued, "You will recollect that a few months after your mother had brought you here you, Lucinda, burst suddenly into this room one morning and begged me to buy an old dolls' house that was for sale in the village. I believe it was one that the carpenter, Robert Pryor, had constructed for his daughter."

"Yes," I said, "Mr. Pryor wanted to sell it because Prue had outgrown it and had come to work here at the Manor."

"Precisely," said Uncle Pescott, "and that reminds me—I have discovered that Prudence has a habit of listening at keyholes. Several times, when I have been giving orders, I have opened the library door suddenly, and found her just outside."

"I expect she was only polishing the floor of the corridor," I said.

"That is what she told me," said Uncle Pescott, "but I

believe she was lying. I believe she has a great reputation as a gossip. Tell me, Lucinda—you probably hear things that are kept from me—is she not known as Prying Prue?"

"Uncle Pescott," I said, "you were going to tell me something."

"Not so fast," said Uncle Pescott. "We'll clarify this matter first, if you please. Have you or your sisters ever caught this girl listening outside a door?"

"No," I said.

Suddenly the library had grown hateful and I wanted to get away.

We all know that Prue talks a great deal, in fact she seems never to stop talking. Her cheeks grow red and her prominent eyes shine with pleasure when she has anything extraordinary to relate, but she is good-hearted and kind and devoted to Mamma.

"I must remember to tell your mother to speak to Prudence," said Uncle Pescott. "What became of the dolls' house?"

"Miss Alder bought it," I said.

"Indeed!" said Uncle Pescott. "And why should a village dressmaker want a dolls' house? Miss Alder is an eccentric old maid, but——"

"She's not so very old," I said, "and she bought it for the Baby House. That's the tiny cottage that is attached to her cottage. The village children are allowed to go and play with the dolls' house."

"If the village children are not at school they should be out in the fields scaring the birds or helping their parents at home," said Uncle Pescott sharply. "Poor children should not be encouraged to play. The earlier they learn to work the better. I believe I must have a word with Miss Alder. She has a certain quickness of understanding that is unusual in country people. I have heard that she once lived in London. That would account for her superiority."

"I cannot imagine what we or the village people would do without Miss Alder," I said.

"Indeed!" said Uncle Pescott. "Indeed! You would do well, Lucinda, to be a little less warm in your commendations. Miss Alder is, no doubt, an admirable woman but she is, after all, only one of the villagers. And you are a niece of the Squire."

"She is our kindest friend," I said.

But Uncle Pescott was still speaking, "Since I have broached the subject," he said, "I must tell you, Lucinda, that you and the boys treat the villagers in too familiar a manner. As so many of them work on the estate and at the Manor, it is extremely bad for discipline."

"But *we* work at the Manor too," I said.

"That is an entirely different matter," said Uncle Pescott.

"You were going to tell me something, Uncle Pescott," I said.

I longed to return to the school-room but knew that, for Mamma's sake, I must remain quiet and polite.

Uncle Pescott placed himself in front of me. "You may inform your brothers and sisters," he said, "that I intend to seek out the finest cabinet-maker in London and instruct him to build a dolls' house."

Chapter 2

PROTEST IN THE LIBRARY

FOR SEVERAL SECONDS I BELIEVE I SIMPLY STARED AT UNCLE Pescott in silence. I was so astonished I could think of nothing to say.

Years before, when we were little children and had longed for a dolls' house to play with, I—being more stupid than my sisters—had dared to ask him to buy us the village dolls' house and had received an absolute refusal and a severe rebuke.

Now, when we were all too old for such a toy, Uncle Pescott proposed to give us one.

"Well?" said Uncle Pescott. "Well? Have you lost the use of your tongue, Lucinda?"

I collected my wits. "Uncle Pescott," I said, "Flora is sixteen and a half and Isabella is fifteen. And I'm thirteen today. We are almost young ladies and too old to play with a dolls' house. As for George and Harry—they'd never look at it."

"Precisely," said Uncle Pescott. "That is what I assumed. My dolls' house will not be used for play."

"I don't understand," I said. "What is it for?"

"It will be a model of the Manor," said Uncle Pescott, "a small, exact copy, perfect in scale and detail. I have been contemplating some such project for a considerable time. At first I intended to give orders to some artist for four paintings of the Manor to be executed from north, south, east and west. But it struck me that even then certain aspects of the house—the north-west and south-east for instance—would receive scant justice. A complete model will, of course, solve every problem. The Manor will be seen in its entirety."

"It seems a curious idea," I said.

"Curious and, I flatter myself, delightful," said Uncle Pescott. "I heard, only the other day, that Lord Elliston had presented his two young daughters with a dolls' kitchen, complete with every kind of kettle and stewpan. His girls are, I believe, far younger than you and will, doubtless, enjoy playing at cooking and washing the dishes in the safe knowledge that they will never have actually to perform such tasks. Our model will be more ambitious."

"But won't it cost a great deal of money?" I asked.

"I am prepared for a very substantial outlay," said Uncle Pescott. "No expense will be spared. I feel it my duty to let nothing stand in the way of perfect achievement. When, nine years ago, I heard of the death of Sir James Pescott, with his wife and two sons, in that dreadful carriage accident, I knew where my duty lay—I knew that I must make every sacrifice to add articles of taste, refinement and beauty to the contents of the Manor, and thus add lustre to our name. Had your father lived he might have assisted me and borne part of this heavy responsibility—although he never showed the smallest interest in our forbears or our living relatives."

"Papa was too busy teaching the young ladies in London to play the pianoforte," I said.

"I believe I was not idle in London either," said Uncle Pescott, "but I always venerated our family name. You may recollect, Lucinda, that I once showed you the remarkable sketch I made, at the age of seventeen, of our Family Tree. I should have had that sketch framed if the mice in my London lodgings had not devoured a good part of it. But that gives

16

me an idea. I must certainly look for some artist to re-draw it for me. It would look admirable over this fireplace."

"But I still can't understand the use of the dolls' house," I said. "The Manor itself stands here, for everyone to see, so why should a model be necessary?"

"The word 'use' is not relevant to my intentions," said Uncle Pescott. "The building of the dolls' house will be an act of piety. I am well aware that models of other noble English residences have been constructed before, but I believe mine will surpass them all. And Lord and Lady Elliston and the Honourable Mrs. Billing and our other neighbours will see that the Squire of Rindle Green has both excellent taste and the means to gratify it."

Since we have almost no visitors in our isolated part of the valley and Lord and Lady Elliston have never called and the Honourable Mrs. Billing only once, it seemed unlikely that Uncle Pescott's taste would be greatly admired.

I had listened quietly but now a kind of desperation took possession of me. I looked down at my slippers. I had fitted new pieces of cardboard into them only that morning because there was a hole in each sole and they could no longer be repaired. "Uncle Pescott," I said, "may I speak freely to you?"

"By all means," said Uncle Pescott. "I am still waiting for your comments or, may I say, congratulations?"

"We all need new shoes," I said.

I saw his face change and hurried on before he could speak. "And our clothes are almost worn out. This frock I'm wearing was Isabella's and before that it was Flora's. It was made from one of the dresses Mamma brought when she came here and now the sleeves are so patched I must wear a jacket to hide them. And look, Uncle Pescott, look at my shoes!"

"Those are your mother's business," said Uncle Pescott.

"Everything we wear—our petticoats and stockings, our bonnets and gloves, even our handkerchiefs are old," I said. "And night after night Mamma sits up darning and patching

17

because she has no time during the day. I've seen her candle-light under the door, and sometimes she doesn't get to bed until two o'clock. As for the boys' clothes—I know she is almost in despair about them."

"I am scarcely responsible for the boys growing out of their clothes," said Uncle Pescott.

"For years," I said, "Miss Alder has brought us all the scraps of silk and lace and ribbon that were left when she had completed the different dresses for her customers. She has also done us another kindness—she has disposed of nearly all the trinkets and ornaments that Mamma had when she came here. Miss Alder had sold them among her customers and brought Mamma the money. Mamma has nothing left now but her locket and her wedding ring."

Uncle Pescott would have interrupted but I gave him no chance. "D'you know that the villagers talk about our poor clothes and our poverty?" I said. "I believe they pity us because they know we're not to blame. But I've seen them smile when one of us appears with a new collar on a patched dress or in an old bonnet with fresh ribbons. We could make our own dresses, with Miss Alder's help, if you'd give us a little money to buy the stuff. But what can we do when we've no money at all? Mamma's trinket money has all been spent on shoes and boots, and now there's not a penny left. So what can we do, Uncle Pescott? What can we do?"

"So the villagers smile, do they?" said Uncle Pescott. "They smile at your clothes. Which villagers?"

But I left the question unanswered. "You say you'll build a dolls' house and no expense will be spared," I cried, "but Mamma works like some poor slave and you pay her nothing. Before Mamma came to the Manor no housekeeper stayed more than a few months, but Mamma has stayed for seven years."

I was aware that I was shouting but was too enraged to lower my voice.

"You talk of our forbears," I cried, "but they're dead, buried in the churchyard in their great stone tombs. We're living, Uncle Pescott, we're living! And you force us to see our Mamma exhausted with overwork and anxiety and growing paler every day. And you treat us like beggars—and that is what we've become." I stopped, trembling.

"Have you finished?" said Uncle Pescott and I nodded.

"You have said enough," said Uncle Pescott. "More than enough. I had thought to give pleasure with the announcement of my intentions but now I forbid you to mention the dolls' house to anyone. Do you understand? The matter is to be kept entirely secret. As for your behaviour—your mother will hear of that at once. Were you a boy, I should whip you for your impertinence. You may go."

He turned his back on me and I was shaking so dreadfully that I could scarcely cross the room and open the door.

I nearly fell over Prue, who was kneeling outside in the corridor with her polish and polishing cloths.

I shut the door quickly.

"You should keep away from all doors, Prue," I said. "Especially when my Uncle is on the other side."

So now I am in disgrace.

I told Mamma everything, as far as I could, without actually mentioning the dolls' house, and she did not reproach me. She only said, "We must guard our tongue, Lucinda, while we live here. Perhaps one day we shall have a home of our own."

Then Uncle Pescott sent for her and she had to hurry away.

"You are so stupid, Luce," said Flora and she took me by the shoulders and began to shake me. "Stupid. Stupid! Now Uncle Pescott will shout at poor Mamma and she'll get one of her headaches. You should have thought of that—but you never think. Stupid!"

"If you shake me any more," I said, "I shall be sick."

"Luce shouldn't be sick on her birthday," said Harry, who is very tender-hearted.

Flora took her hands off my shoulders. "I'd forgotten it was your birthday," she said.

"So had I," I said.

Chapter 3

THE FIVE BEDROOMS

A WEEK HAS PASSED AND THIS MORNING UNCLE PESCOTT DROVE to Ramsford to catch the train for London. He will stay in his London house for several days.

I believe he has gone to look for a cabinet-maker to construct the dolls' house but I have said nothing of this to Mamma and the others. We have all been wonderfully cheerful since Uncle Pescott left.

I have been looking at the Manor with different eyes since I know it will be the model for a dolls' house.

The Rindle Valley is almost enclosed by wooded hills. The Rindle, which is little more than a wide stream, rises in these hills, twists along the valley between grassy banks and then forms a loop round our village of Rindle Green, a mile from the Manor gates. The Manor itself, which was built about 1720, stands on a slope at the end of the valley with its gardens and orchard stretching up the hill behind it. Its long drive curves down to the stony road which begins at the Manor gates and runs to the village and then on to Rindlebridge. Rindlebridge is situated near the mouth of the valley where the London Road cuts across it. The village of Reyne is five miles away and Ramsford is seven, but Ramsford is so large that it is almost a town. It has a Grammar School and a railway station and Lord Elliston owns a great house on the far side of it. All the woods and meadows that we can see from the Manor windows belong to Uncle Pescott. It is strange that he should have so much and we so little.

In the old days, Miss Alder says, when Sir James Pescott was alive, month after month carriages followed each other along the road to the Manor and the house was crowded with guests all the year round. In the summer there were picnics in the woods, day-long carriage excursions and archery on the lawn. And in the winter there was skating on the Rindle, with dancing and music in the evenings. Sir James detested London, so his many friends had always to visit him in the country.

Christmas was the climax of the year. The Manor overflowed with guests and at night so many candles burned in the great rooms that the Manor shone like a beacon in the dark valley. I should have loved to see it.

Not everything has changed since Uncle Pescott came. He complains, each year, about the ruinous expenses of Christmas, but the waits still tramp from the village and play outside in the drive and the village boys sing carols under the school-room windows. And there is a kind of joy and excitement in the air at Christmas that not even Uncle Pescott can spoil.

Mamma is now so taken up with preparations for Christmas that our lessons with her have had to be given up until after the New Year. It is a sorrow to us all, because our afternoon hours in the school-room (which is also our parlour and dining-room) are the only times when we can all sit quietly together. In the evenings after supper, when most ordinary families can be comfortable, round the fire, Flora, Isabella and I must do our housework.

There are five unused bedrooms at the Manor and they have old-fashioned fourposter beds and a great number of carved chests and wardrobes. And we have to clean these rooms. It is our duty to shake out the bed curtains and polish all the furniture once a week, but we may only do this when the servants, who live in the village, have returned to their homes and those few who sleep at the Manor have retired to their attics for the night. They usually do this about eight o'clock.

The five rooms are kept locked during the day and nobody is supposed to know that we have charge of them because Uncle Pescott considers it unfitting that it should be known that his relatives do housework. On one night a week—we never know which night—Uncle Pescott comes with a lamp, to inspect the rooms and see that no speck of dust is clinging to the furniture and no secret moth hiding in the bed curtains. When he has finished his inspection he returns to the library fire while we replace the dust sheets and carry the keys back to Mamma. Our brooms, polish and dusters are always left locked in the largest room.

I believe it is right that we should work, but I wish we could do it when Mamma herself is busy with the house-keeping.

Chapter 4

CHRISTMAS

CHRISTMAS DAY. IT IS A COLD, GLITTERING DAY. FLORA AND Isabella talked, in bed, so late last night, that I was kept awake and got up with a headache. So Mamma said that I was to stay at home quietly until they and Uncle Pescott all returned from Church.

Now I have the school-room and the whole of Christmas morning to myself.

On Christmas Day we all dine with Uncle Pescott after the morning service and I shall be glad when the meal is over. It is always uncomfortable and today, since Uncle Pescott still refuses to speak to me, it will be more uncomfortable than usual. I shall wish him "A Merry Christmas" but I expect he will not reply.

Yesterday the Yule Log was brought down from the woods where it had been lying all the summer. Ropes had been fastened round it and four of our strongest men half-dragged and half-rolled it down the slope of High Meadow and through the orchard gate.

We and all the servants ran out to see it brought through the garden and the maids curtsied as it passed and the men touched their foreheads. This was because all the villagers believe that the Yule Log is full of good omens.

Flora, Isabella and I curtsied too, because it was a joyous

occasion, and George and Harry rushed forward to help pull it. It burned in the library all day.

I have been told by Miss Alder that Sir James Pescott believed in all the old traditions and every Christmas Eve spiced ale was heated over the Yule Log and all the village was welcome to come to the Manor and drink from the wassail-bowl. Those who drank were supposed to forget their feuds and quarrels. It is a pity that Uncle Pescott and I could not have drunk from a wassail-bowl and then perhaps he would have spoken to me again. But there has been no wassail at the Manor since he came. The Yule Log must never be allowed to burn entirely away. Every year, part of it must be saved and stored in a safe place until the following Christmas, when it must be used to light the new Yule Log. The villagers believe this is a security against fire in the house—but I have no idea why.

There was no decorated tree for the village children this Christmas but the mummers came in the evening and Miss Alder came with them. It is she who rehearses their parts with them and renovates their costumes. They call her the "Mistress of the Mummers"—which seems a curious title for a village dressmaker. Even Uncle Pescott cannot refuse to receive the mummers.

We were called down to the library at eight o'clock. A semicircle of chairs had been set for us and we sat down quietly with Mamma while the servants gathered behind us.

Uncle Pescott remained sitting at his desk.

The Yule Log still burned on the hearth and the library was warm and bright because extra lamps had been carried in.

I looked across at Uncle Pescott. Sometimes I feel that his silence is like a small, icy stone that I must carry with me wherever I go. It is terrible when two living creatures never speak to each other. But Uncle Pescott was still writing and never looked in our direction.

There was a sudden clatter in the corridor and a drum was banged softly outside the door. Then Miss Alder came in smiling and the mummers followed her, looking wild and strange in Uncle Pescott's library. They all had masks, and their smocks were sewn with scraps of bright material and knots of ribbons. One by one, they stepped forward and introduced themselves.

The first was Father Christmas, who carried a holly branch and a sprig of mistletoe; the second was the Grand Turk, who wore a great round turban and carried a wooden scimitar; the third was Saint George, in a helmet that looked like a pudding basin. He had both a wooden sword and a spear. The fourth was Little Jolly Jack, who showed us his curious musical instrument, made from a pig's bladder, and told us it was his hurdy-gurdy; the fifth was the Doctor, with a box of pills as big as a bonnet box under his arm; and the sixth and last was the Dragon. We always like the Dragon best. He had a crocodile mask and carried a red umbrella and was always falling over his long, stuffed tail which was tied round his waist under his smock.

Each of these curious characters recited a rhyme and bowed very politely and we clapped loudly, although we had hardly understood a word they said. Miss Alder can never persuade the mummers to speak slowly, and they gabble their sentences behind their masks, and scarcely pause for breath, so that we seem to be listening to some unknown, foreign language.

It was, however, soon clear that Saint George and the Grand Turk had begun to quarrel. They waved their weapons and shouted and shook their fists, and finally Saint George flung down his glove.

The Grand Turk could not, at first, find his glove and Miss Alder had to make signs that it was in one of his breeches' pockets. Even then, it took him a considerable time to discover it and we had to bury our faces in our handkerchiefs to hide our laughter. The Dragon was so overcome with

merriment that he began to stamp about the library and fell over his tail. He landed on all fours and his umbrella flew across the room.

I dared not look at Uncle Pescott. At last, when we were almost breathless behind our handkerchiefs and George and Harry had began to shout advice and encouragement to the poor Turk, he found his glove and tossed it into Saint George's face.

And the fight began.

This is the part of the play that the boys particularly enjoy and it was clear that Saint George and the Grand Turk enjoyed it too.

Their wooden weapons clattered together again and again as they leapt from side to side, rushed at each other, retreated and then attacked again. I believe they would have continued their battle till midnight if Miss Alder had not clapped her hands. Then the Turk dropped his scimitar and Saint George stuck his sword carefully under the Turk's left arm. The poor Turk uttered a fearful groan and lay on his back, so we knew that Saint George had won.

He stepped forward and pulled off his mask and we recognized him as one of the young farm labourers who work at the Manor Farm. He was panting a little and I heard Miss Alder say, "Take your time, Billy," but the fight seemed to have given him confidence because he took a deep breath and began to bellow:

> "Ladies and Gentlemen,
> You've seen what I've done
> I've cut this Turk down
> Like the evening sun.
> Is there any Doctor that can be found
> To cure this knight of his deadly wound?"

Then the Doctor rushed forward and assured us that he could cure every kind of pain.

28

> *"The pains within, the pains without,*
> *The rip, the pip, the palsy and the gout."*

The Dragon, who had picked himself up and retrieved his umbrella, asked what the Doctor's pills were made of and the Doctor replied, "The liver and lights of an old buck flea."

This line always delighted George and Harry, who began to clap and drum with their heels and were hushed into silence by Mamma.

The Doctor knelt down, opened his huge pill box and took out a pill as big as a penny and administered it to the poor Turk. (Miss Alder makes the pills, which are really little biscuits.)

No sooner had he eaten it than the Turk sat up, straightened his mask, which had slipped over one ear, and got to his feet. Then we felt we really had cause to applaud.

But this was not the end. Little Jolly Jack had turned away and pulled off his mask.

When he turned back to us we saw his face was entirely black with burnt cork and Harry cried, "Beelzebub! Beelzebub!"

"Yes, sir, that's me," said Beelzebub, grinning. He was one of the cowmen from the Manor Farm. Then he recited his rhyme, which we all knew,

> *"Here come I, Beelzebub,*
> *Over my shoulder I carry a club,*
> *Under my arm a dripping pan,*
> *Don't I look a nice young man?"*

"No you don't," shouted Harry. "You've got a dirty face."

At this point there is usually another fight—between Saint George and Beelzebub—but Uncle Pescott had taken out his watch and was looking at it and frowning.

"It's growing late," he said, "and I think we've seen enough."

For a moment there was silence and the warm library seemed to grow cold. The mummers stood still, waiting to be told what to do, and Mamma half-rose in her chair and then sat down again.

"But this isn't the end," cried Harry. "This isn't the end. There's another fight."

"It must be the end, for this year," said Miss Alder.

So the Doctor took the lid off his pill box and gave it to Father Christmas, who recited the last rhyme.

> "*Ladies and gentlemen,*
> *Our story is ended.*
> *Our money-box is recommended;*
> *Five or six shillings will do us no harm*
> *Silver or copper or gold if you can.*"

Then he brought the lid to us and we put in the sixpences that Mamma had saved and given to us before we came downstairs. Uncle Pescott put in a small coin and then the servants pressed forward with their pennies.

Miss Alder opened the library door and stood aside and the mummers jostled out into the corridor. One of them must have kicked the drum because there was a loud hollow boom like thunder.

"A Happy Christmas!" said Miss Alder and curtsied in the doorway.

Mamma followed her hurriedly out of the room. Uncle Pescott turned to the servants.

"Clear the chairs away as quickly as you can," he said. "I still have work to do."

Prue called out, "The men has to take the Yule Log, sir. It's nearly burnt through."

"It must wait until I have gone to bed," said Uncle Pescott. "I was nearly suffocated with the smoke last year."

I had to go back to the library ten minutes later, to search for the Turk's glove, which had been borrowed from the

Rector. Uncle Pescott did not look up when I begged his pardon for disturbing him. I found the glove and would have gone quietly away, but something made me pause.

"Uncle Pescott," I said, "you've not spoken to me since my birthday. And it's Christmas Eve. Do you think——"

"I believe it is past your bedtime. Please shut the door," said Uncle Pescott.

So I closed the door without another word.

Chapter 5

PRUE KNOCKS AT THE DOOR

TODAY IS DECEMBER 28TH AND IT IS STILL VERY COLD. THE WATER in our water jugs was frozen this morning and we had to stand them by the school-room fire to melt the ice. The fire itself has been smoking dreadfully and it is difficult to keep warm. How I long for the spring.

I have been with Uncle Pescott. Suddenly, he sent for me and I went at once, trembling a little and yet glad that, at last, he wished to speak to me.

He had a great roll of old, stiff papers on his desk and had flattened down one of them with a book at each corner.

He said, "Come here" and then pointed at this paper. "Do you know what that is?" he asked.

"It's a drawing of the front of the Manor," I said.

"It's the front elevation," said Uncle Pescott. "Now look at this."

He unrolled another sheet and carefully weighted it down.

"It's a kind of plan," I said.

"It's the plan of the whole of this floor," said Uncle Pescott.

"Yes," I said. "It's extremely neat."

"It's considerably more than that," said Uncle Pescott, sharply. "It's drawn exactly to scale."

"Yes," I said.

"There is everything here," said Uncle Pescott, taking up

the roll. "Everything! Plans and elevations, details of doors and windows, of chimneys and mouldings with every measurement clearly marked. The papers are a little brown and spotted but that's of no consequence. I imagine the architect submitted all these drawings to Sir James Pescott's great-grandfather when the Manor was built. The Rector once mentioned having seen them so I knew they must be here. But I've only just discovered them, on the shelf behind the works of Samuel Johnson. This library is ridiculously over-crowded with books."

"You must be very pleased, Uncle Pescott," I said.

"I am relieved, greatly relieved," said Uncle Pescott. "These drawings are precisely what I require for the cabinet-maker who is to construct the dolls' house."

I understood then why Uncle Pescott had sent for me. He wished to make it clear that nothing I had said had affected his purpose.

"I intend to have the small parlour cleared of furniture and turned into a workshop," said Uncle Pescott. "I intend to keep everything under my own eye and I shall watch the work as it progresses and make my comments. The cabinet-maker will arrive from London the day after tomorrow. He will sleep at the Lodge and have all his meals here in his work-shop. I am not anxious for the village gossips to get into conversation with him and I shall see that Prudence Pryor has no contact with him. The normal scale for dolls' houses is, I believe, one inch to a foot but, since the Manor is large, I shall insist on a slightly smaller scale. Have you spoken of my project to anyone?"

Uncle Pescott shot this last question at me as though he wished to catch me off my guard.

"No," I said.

"Not even to your mother?"

"No," I said. "May I go now, Uncle Pescott?"

"The other night," said Uncle Pescott, "you appeared to

wish to speak to me. Well? What is it you wished to say?"

I looked at him and felt the same anger that I had felt when he had talked of the dolls' house before. George's coat is too small for him and should be passed on to Harry, but then George would have no warm coat, and Mamma's walking shoes can no longer be repaired and let in the damp.

"Well?" said Uncle Pescott.

"I think you would not listen to me, Uncle Pescott," I said. "May I go away now?"

"You may go when I tell you to go," said Uncle Pescott. "You mentioned some time ago, that the villagers laughed when you wore new ribbons in your bonnets. Which villagers?"

"No one laughed," I said.

"You said they laughed when you wore new ribbons or a new collar," said Uncle Pescott sharply.

"I said I saw some of them smile. That is a different thing, Uncle Pescott," I said.

"Laughing or smiling—it's only a matter of degree," said Uncle Pescott. "Who smiled, then?"

"It's so long since any of us has worn anything new," I said, "I'm afraid I don't remember, Uncle Pescott."

"You mean you choose to forget?"

I remained silent.

"The villagers represent the lower orders at their worst," said Uncle Pescott. "They are dull-witted, uncouth and totally lacking in every quality that may be called 'gentlemanly'. Consideration for them is misplaced. You will tell me which of them dared to smile. And you will tell me *now*."

"No," I said.

"You must understand," shouted Uncle Pescott, who always shouts when he is angry, "you must understand that I will not permit either myself or my relatives to become laughing-stocks. I abhor stupid laughter and despise those who indulge in it. Do you understand that, Lucinda? Those

34

without education laugh to hide their ignorance; those without sense laugh because others laugh. I exempt Miss Alder from these strictures because she is a Londoner and has a kind of intelligence. Now—which of the villagers dared to smile? Tell me and I shall know how to deal with them."

He picked up a long ruler and began to turn it in his fingers.

"I like laughing, Uncle Pescott," I said, and heard my voice shake because I was afraid he meant to hit me.

"You laugh because you are an immature child," shouted Uncle Pescott. "Have you ever heard me laugh?"

"No," I said, "never."

"Tell me which of the villagers dared to smile," cried Uncle Pescott.

"I don't remember," I said. "I don't remember. Please let me go, Uncle Pescott."

"You shall go when you have told me—only then," said Uncle Pescott, and he made the ruler whistle through the air as though he were testing its strength.

"Let me go, Uncle Pescott," I said, and then I shut my eyes quickly because I thought he was going to strike me.

(I know many children are beaten when they are young but Mamma has always been gentle with us. And I was afraid.)

"You refuse to tell me then?" said Uncle Pescott, and at that moment there was a loud, sudden knock on the library door.

I opened my eyes quickly and Uncle Pescott put down the ruler. Then he called, "Come in" in so furious a voice that, had I been on the other side of the door, I should have run away. But the door opened, and there was Prue, red-faced and beaming as usual. She curtsied to Uncle Pescott.

"Tom wants to know, sir," she said, "if you was wantin' another basket of logs brought in. It's a cold mornin', sir, and Tom thought——"

"The fire was made up half an hour ago," said Uncle Pescott angrily.

35

"And could Miss Luce come now, sir?" said Prue. "Her Mamma's been wonderin' where she were and askin' for her."

"Very well. You may go, Lucinda," said Uncle Pescott, and began to roll together his papers. His brows were drawn together and his face was red with anger. Prue crossed the room, took my hand and hurried me out of the room. As soon as we were in the corridor, she closed the library door and then turned and shook her fist at it.

"It's him as should have his face blacked with cork," she whispered. "It 'ud come natural to *him* to play Beelzebub. One of these days, Miss Luce——"

"Prue, where *is* Mamma?" I asked.

"I don't know, Miss Luce," said Prue.

"But you said——" I began.

"I just happened to be outside the door," said Prue, "and us in the village knows who our friends is."

Chapter 6

MRS. MARDEN

TODAY, I SAW POOR MRS. MARDEN.
In very cold weather she leaves her hut in the woods and comes down to sleep in the hayloft over our stables. The horses pay no attention to her, she is quite harmless and no one tells Uncle Pescott she is there. He would certainly send her away if he knew. She is a piteous, foolish woman who used to live in the village, and she wears old ragged black clothes and a broken bonnet. Her complexion is as dark as a gypsy's and she has no shoes or stockings. I suppose they wore out long ago.

Day after day, summer and winter, she waits on the Green for her daughter to come home and night after night she tramps back along the carriage road with perhaps half a loaf or some cold potatoes in her basket, that the villagers have put out for her to find. She will accept nothing from the hand of any human creature.

I met her early this morning, at the end of our drive, hurrying towards the road. The rags of her skirts were flapping about her ankles and she was looking neither to right nor to left. I stepped aside, but she saw me and turned quickly. "Sophie!" she said and then, "Ah, no. I beg your pardon, Miss. I thought you were my girl. I'm going to the village to meet her now. Who are *you*, Miss?"

"I'm Lucinda," I said. "I live here."

"Ah, yes," she said. "Ah, yes. I've heard tell of you, Miss. They call you 'Miss Luce'. You feature my Sophie, but she's taller and prettier than you. She'll be waiting for me now so I must hurry. Good morning, Miss."

And she pulled the hood of her old cloak over her bonnet and strode away.

Miss Alder once told me Mrs. Marden's story, and it is so sad that I can scarcely write it without tears. Mrs. Marden is the widow of one of Sir James Pescott's gamekeepers, who was killed, years ago, in a fight with poachers. In those days, more than thirty years ago, the game laws were both ridiculous and cruel, but poor labourers often turned poachers to earn a little extra money by secretly selling the game to poulterers or taverns. So fights between poachers and gamekeepers were not unusual.

Sir James Pescott settled seventy pounds a year on Mrs. Marden, after her husband's death, so her daughter Sophie, who was then a little child, was able to go to school at Rindlebridge when she grew older and stay until she was fourteen. She was a pretty, gay young girl and, as soon as she left school, she went as a parlour-maid to the Manor, where she became a favourite with everyone.

Mrs. Marden was very religious and very careful with her money. She set aside every penny she could save of the seventy pounds so that Sophie might have a little fortune when she married. But Sophie, who continued to live in their cottage in the village, grew anxious because her mother spent so little on food and necessities.

Almost every night, she brought Mrs. Marden some tit-bit from the Manor kitchens—a piece of pie, perhaps, or a few little cakes or a slice of meat. Sophie said the housekeeper had sent them.

The girl greatly loved her mother and once even knocked at Miss Alder's door and begged her to speak to Mrs. Marden.

"My mother eats scarce enough to keep a bird alive," she

said. "She'll die to make me a rich orphan." And poor Sophie burst into tears.

Miss Alder went to see Mrs. Marden and Mrs. Marden listened politely to everything Miss Alder said.

"Sophie lives in constant anxiety about you," said Miss Alder.

"God has given me seventy pounds a year and a dear child," said Mrs. Marden. "What else should I do but save for her? I've no one else."

One day, when Sophie had been working at the Manor for about two years, there was a sudden fierce thunderstorm, one late afternoon, after a day of bright sunshine. Sophie had left the village in the morning without her cloak or wooden pattens, and was, besides, terrified of thunder. So Mrs. Marden set out for the Manor with Sophie's things in a basket. She intended to wait until Sophie had finished her work and then bring her home.

There were guests at the Manor as usual and when Mrs. Marden arrived at the main kitchen entrance, she was told that the Squire and his guests were dining and Sophie was helping to wait at table and would be occupied for some time. Mrs. Marden asked if she might sit down and was given a chair. As she sat in the Manor kitchen she recollected all the delicacies that Sophie had brought her and sent a message of thanks to the housekeeper who, being an elderly lady, was rarely seen in the village.

The servant who took the message seemed puzzled, but went away to find the housekeeper and returned, almost at once, to ask Mrs. Marden to step into the housekeeper's room.

Then it appeared that no pie or cakes or meat had ever been sent to Mrs. Marden and that Sophie had, in fact, been stealing them. The housekeeper was not unkind. She knew that Sophie worried continuously about her mother's health and she had heard of the almost miserly way in which Mrs. Marden hoarded her money, so she said that the thieving must, of course, stop at once, but that as Sophie was a good worker, and Mrs. Marden herself was the Squire's pensioner, nothing would be said about the matter to the Squire and Sophie would be allowed to stay.

Mrs. Marden appeared deeply distressed and returned to the village at once; Sophie was sent home early. (Miss Alder heard all this from the housekeeper later.)

That night, about eleven o'clock, Miss Alder was wakened up by a knocking at her door. It was pitch dark, the village candles were all out and Miss Alder could not at first see who was waiting on the step.

It was Sophie.

Miss Alder brought her into the warm kitchen, put fresh wood on the fire and made some tea. She said she had no idea then what Sophie's trouble was, but the girl was white-faced and shivering. She drank the tea without a word and then began, slowly, to tell Miss Alder the whole story.

"My mother says I've shamed her before God and the whole village," she said. "Yet what I took I took only for her. She would never allow me to buy her anything.

"Every day enough food is prepared at the Manor to feed the whole village for a week and every night enough is thrown into the pig buckets to provide my mother with all she could eat in a fortnight. I could not endure the thought that my mother was going hungry when there was so much waste at the Manor.

"The Squire's an open-handed gentleman who gives to all who ask, but my mother would never have forgiven me if I'd asked anything for her. She's very proud and she's not poor, so how could I have begged for a few tarts or slices of cake?

"With my mother's seventy pounds and the ten pounds a year that I earn we could have been very comfortable. But my mother says I've shamed her, so I'm going away."

For a long time that night Miss Alder talked to Sophie and promised to go herself, as soon as it was light, and speak to Mrs. Marden.

Sophie sat leaning over the fire and shivering and only said, "My mother called me a thief and I *am* a thief. My mother said I've shamed her, so I'm going away."

Miss Alder told me she was almost in despair, but when the clock struck one, Sophie suddenly stood up and said she was going home. Miss Alder lighted a lantern and walked with her back to Mrs. Marden's cottage and Sophie opened the door very softly so as not to disturb her mother and turned, for an instant, before she went upstairs, to smile at Miss Alder.

In the morning she had gone.

A week later Miss Alder received a brief letter from her. She had walked to Ramsford that night and caught the early morning coach to London, and had gone into service at Lord Elliston's great London house. She intended never to return to Rindle Green. She asked Miss Alder to tell Mrs. Marden this and to see that she saved no more of the pension money.

"I want for nothing," Sophie wrote, "and I should not, in any case, take a penny of the money. Pray be kind to my mother."

Miss Alder went at once to see Mrs. Marden, but she put her head out of the window, and begged not to be disturbed. She was wearing her black Sunday clothes and said she was saying her prayers. She received Sophie's message in silence.

Miss Alder wrote to Sophie, but had no reply. So she wrote to old Lady Elliston, whom she knew quite well.

Lady Elliston answered at once, that Sophie had already left but that neither the housekeeper nor any of the servants knew where she had gone.

Then Miss Alder herself travelled to London, but could find no trace of Sophie and, at last, returned to Rindle Green.

Mrs. Marden remained in her cottage for several weeks. She continued to wear her Sunday clothes, but she cleaned her doorstep and polished her windows as usual. And she made her small purchases at the village shop and went to church on Sundays. But she hardly spoke to anyone.

Then she vanished.

No one knew where she had gone and no one saw her until, about three months later, she appeared, early one morning, outside the village and told everyone who passed that she was waiting for her daughter.

"My Sophie tried to feed me as God's ravens fed Elijah," she said. "She's a good girl. She'll be coming soon. Have you seen her?"

All day she stopped the villagers with the same question, "Have you seen my Sophie?", and she spoke quietly and politely, but her aspect was so wild that no one knew how to answer her. Somebody would have run for Miss Alder, but she was staying at Lord Elliston's house at Ramsford, to make new dresses for old Lady Elliston, who always spent part of the year in London and part in the country.

When evening came Mrs. Marden turned from the village and walked away along the stony road that leads to the Manor, and Mr. Pryor, Prue's father, followed her at a distance because the villagers, who felt she was still one of themselves, feared she might do herself some harm. Mr. Pryor followed her past the Manor, up the slope of High Meadow and into the woods. It was almost dark when, stepping quietly after her from tree to tree, he saw her creep into the tent of branches that she had made in a kind of hollow. She has lived there ever since, except in very cold weather.

The villagers have built a thatched roof over her tent, to keep out the rain, and she sleeps on dry leaves and bracken. And still every day she walks to the village and tells everyone that her daughter is coming.

But Sophie will never come.

About four years after Sophie went away, a stranger called at Miss Alder's cottage. He was a smart young man but his face was pale and miserable and he seemed, at first, scarcely able to speak. He said Sophie had asked him to bring a message.

He was a London footman and he and Sophie had been married for more than three years and had been very happy. "But we went walking, last Tuesday evening, by the Serpentine," he said, "and Sophie must have took a fever. She died last night. She said I was to ask you to be kind to her mother."

Miss Alder begged the young man to come in, but he said he had to return to London at once. So Miss Alder brought him some food, as he stood on the doorstep, and he gave her his address and left soon afterwards.

When Miss Alder tried, as gently as she could, to make Mrs. Marden understand that Sophie would never come back to Rindle Green, Mrs. Marden smiled in her strange way, and only said, "My Sophie won't keep me waiting too long."

Sophie died before Uncle Pescott came to the Manor or I was born. But Mrs. Marden is still waiting.

Chapter 7

A GENTLEMAN WITH TWO CARRIAGES

January 1857

THE CABINET-MAKER ARRIVED SEVERAL DAYS AGO AND IS SHUT away in the small parlour. The parlour curtains are kept drawn, so that no one may look into the room from the outside and he works all day by lamp-light. I caught a glimpse of him when he arrived. He is a thin, humble-looking man with large hands.

"All the parlour chairs is out in the corridor," said Prue, "and the Squire's been fussin' round him like a wasp round a bit o' puddin'. The poor man'll need a deal of patience if he's to stay shut up with only the Squire goin' in and out. I expect you know what the man's come to do, don't you now, Miss Luce?"

"Miss Luce wouldn't tell you if she did know," said Flora. "Miss Luce is very quiet and circumspect these days. Miss Luce writes a great deal and says nothing—we think she's keeping a journal. But you needn't inform the village of that, Prue."

"I keeps a still tongue in my head," said Prue, and Isabella giggled.

44

"It appears that not a soul is to know what's going on," said Flora.

"I'd a mind to dust the chairs in the corridor," said Prue. "I reckoned they was dirty after all that movin' about. But the Squire come out o' the library and shouted at me. The Squire's taken the parlour key and all the man's meals is to be left on a tray outside o' the door."

"Perhaps Uncle Pescott's having an aquarium built," said George hopefully.

"Or an aviary," said Isabella. "Miss Alder says Lord Elliston has one."

"Or maybe the Squire fancies a bit o' music in the evenin's," said Prue, "and the man's makin' a piannyforty for you young ladies. And the Squire's keepin' it quiet to be a surprise."

"That would indeed be a surprise," said Flora. "You know perfectly well, Prue, that there's a pianoforte in the drawing-room and we're not allowed to touch it."

"Oh well," said Prue. "Maybe the Squire's havin' his coffin got ready so he'll not be caught without one. But my Dad could make him a coffin easy enough—and glad to do it. But maybe the Squire wants somethin' special, with satin inside and gold handles. If it's a coffin he's havin' I hope he'll get into it pretty soon and not leave it lyin' round to be dusted every week. You've not said a word, Miss Luce. Maybe you could just——"

"No, Prue," I said.

"Oh, well," said Prue. "It's time I were gettin' along."

"So you *do* know, Luce," said Flora as Prue closed the door. "You know but you won't tell us."

"Uncle Pescott said I was not to tell anyone," I said.

"I can't imagine why Uncle Pescott should take you into his confidence when I'm the eldest," said Flora and moved over to the mantelpiece and glanced at herself in the mirror. "Of course, Mamma should have been told too," she added.

"We should *all* have been told," said Isabella.

45

"Nothing Uncle Pescott does is of any particular interest to me," said Flora. "But I could easily shake the secret out of you. You'd probably cry though, or be sick, wouldn't you, Luce?"

"I should do both," I said.

Flora smiled at her reflection in the glass. "I shall marry young," she said. "In fact, as soon as I can. I believe there will be no great difficulty. I shall marry to get away from the Manor."

(We are all fair-haired and have grey eyes, but Flora is the family beauty.)

"I believe I shall marry young too," said Isabella. She admires Flora so much that she wishes always to do what Flora does.

"So you may as well tell us the secret, Luce," said Flora, "because it's quite unimportant."

"If I told you," I said, "Uncle Pescott would find out and be angry with Mamma."

"There are still some things that Uncle Pescott has never found out," said Flora. "He's never found out what I think of him, and he never will until the day I leave the Manor. *Then* I shall tell him."

I looked at her in astonishment. Flora has always been Mamma's deputy and has insisted that we must treat Uncle Pescott with perfect respect, and that we must be docile, obedient and polite.

Now she stood, flushed and frowning, like some fierce goddess, and I could easily imagine her seizing thunderbolts and drawing down handfuls of lightning to hurl at Uncle Pescott.

"What will you tell him?" asked George.

"I shall tell him that I despise and detest him—and that I've despised and detested him for years," said Flora.

For an instant there was silence in the school-room.

"I despise him because he is suspicious, petty-minded,

46

ridiculous and mean," said Flora. "And I detest him because of the way he treats Mamma. Mamma herself is so gentle and generous that she cannot see how Uncle Pescott exploits her. But I can see. I'm neither gentle nor generous, and for seven years I've held my tongue only because I feared he would send Mamma and all of us away if I dared to speak. But when I marry everything will be changed."

"It'll be changed for *you*," said Isabella. "You'll go away. But we shall be left here."

"I've made my plans," said Flora. "Night after night I lie in bed and arrange everything."

"You've never told me——" began Isabella.

"I'm telling you now," said Flora. "On my wedding day, when I stand on the Manor steps and am about to be helped into my husband's carriage to drive to our new home, I shall turn to Uncle Pescott and say, in the presence of all the guests, everything that I've so often longed to say. I shall speak clearly and slowly. And I shall end by saying that since I've no affection for the Manor and feel nothing but contempt and hatred for its owner I trust I shall never see either again. Then I shall walk down the steps and be driven away."

"But we shall be left," cried Isabella. "We shall be left."

"Ah, no," said Flora, and suddenly she smiled. "You've not heard the whole of my plan. Everything will be perfectly arranged. As I step into my husband's carriage another, larger carriage will drive up and Mamma and all of you, in your wedding clothes, will step into it. And Prue and Tom, who have been watching from the school-room windows, will quickly carry down our old trunks and boxes that have been secretly packed. And, without a word being spoken to Uncle Pescott, the second carriage will follow my carriage down the drive and out of the gates. And none of us will ever return."

"But where shall we go?" asked George.

"To my husband's house, of course," said Flora. "Apartments will already have been prepared. Dear Mamma will be

47

able to sit reading or embroidering every day with nothing to make her anxious or give her headaches. And we shall all be happy together."

"And what will Uncle Pescott do?" asked Harry.

"He'll be left standing on the steps, alone," said Flora. "The guests will turn away from him and the villagers will hurry back to Rindle Green, whispering together and laughing at his discomforture. And ten years, twenty years later they'll still be talking of my wedding day and reminding each other of everything that occurred. And Uncle Pescott will know that nothing has been forgotten. And that nothing ever *will* be forgotten."

"But you've still to find the gentleman with two carriages," said George.

Chapter 8

THE GREEN BEDROOM

SINCE WE CAME TO THE MANOR I HAVE GROWN TO DREAD THE winter. We are so often cold.

I hate frozen washing water and chapped hands. And I hate the smoking school-room fire.

The library and Uncle Pescott's dining-room are kept warm, but Mamma and the rest of us shiver from October to March.

I hate the darkness of winter even more than the cold—the mornings when we breakfast by candlelight, the grey afternoons that sink into twilight at four o'clock and the long silent evenings when there is no light to be seen outside the Manor except the lanterns of the servants returning to the village. When they have gone there is nothing but darkness outside the windows, and the night sky (unless the moon is shining) is only a little less black than the woods and fields that surround us. Then, in our enclosed valley, the country silence seems to shut us off from the rest of the world and the Manor becomes a prison.

I can still remember the bright gaslight in London. The London streets in winter were often slippery with mud, and fog sometimes lay, like a brown blanket, over all the city. But when there was no fog the gaslight shone beautifully on shop windows and street stalls and the hurrying crowds and I loved it because it had driven the dark away.

I believe I have always loved light. Mamma says that when I was a very small child I would sit happily watching a candle flame, for half an hour at a time, and laugh with pleasure when it flickered in the draught. It is curious that my name should mean "Light".

I have been considering my character. I am thirteen and Flora says I am stupid, childish and impetuous. Perhaps I am all these things—I believe one cannot fully judge one's own character. But I think it is also possible that Flora has already forgotten what it is like to be thirteen.

It is a great comfort to live in the midst of one's own family, even if one is criticised, because one can so safely be oneself.

Uncle Pescott was considerably older than our Papa and seems not to belong to our family at all. I believe he disapproved of Papa because Papa refused to sit in an office and preferred to tramp from house to house giving music lessons.

I believe I shall spend the rest of my life writing. I have only just thought of this. I shall write novels and poems.

I have not the smallest wish to look for a gentleman with two carriages and I should hate to waste my time instructing maids, ordering meals or inspecting linen.

There are so few things that ladies can do that I am glad to have made up my mind.

Every morning we settle round the school-room table to do the school-work that Mamma has set for us and Flora, who is in charge of us, permits no talking or even whispering. But when we have completed our reading and learning we may do as we please until our mid-day meal. This is the time when I fly to my journal.

The conversation and general noise made writing difficult in the school-room and Isabella was always trying to look over my shoulder, so, in the end, I retreated to the bedroom that I share with Flora and Isabella, put on my coat and bonnet and settled down with my pencil and notebook. But even there I had no peace because Flora frequently came in to smooth her hair and study her face in the mirror. And Isabella always followed her.

So I had no choice but to discover another writing place and I now write in one of the great bedrooms that we clean at night. Mamma does not keep the keys of these bedrooms with the other household keys but separately, in the drawer of a small table in the school-room, where we also keep pencils and pens. Uncle Pescott has duplicate keys.

I was trembling when I first took a key and let myself into the bedroom, and saw it by daylight, with its great curtained bed and draped dust sheets. It looked like a room full of hump-backed ghosts. But it was not the shrouded furniture that made me afraid—we had seen it often enough by candlelight—but the fact that I had unlocked the door and entered the room without Uncle Pescott's permission.

I would have asked Mamma and she would possibly have given me the key herself, but if Uncle Pescott had discovered she had done this he would certainly have been angry with her. As it is—if Uncle Pescott does find out what I am doing only I can be blamed. (I am trying very hard to be less impetuous and to consider the effect of all my actions.)

The five bedrooms are at the back of the Manor and not immediately adjacent to the school-room, which is in the front, and I have told Flora that I have found a writing place but hope she will allow me to keep it secret.

When I told her she looked at me smiling and said, "What a child you still are, Luce!"

But she asked no questions.

Flora has grown somewhat absent-minded lately and often stands by the school-room window, for minutes on end, staring down the drive towards the road. Sometimes she sighs and sometimes gives her head a little shake as though she were shaking out thoughts that disturbed her. But always she reminds me of a lady locked in some high tower and longing to escape.

I suppose she is watching for the gentleman with two carriages.

She will be seventeen in May.

My writing room has windows that overlook the terrace, the garden and the long orchard that runs uphill beyond the garden; the bed has curtains of faded green brocade, and the wallpaper, which must be at least twenty years old, is covered with bouquets of moss roses, tulips and spotted iris. At first I could scarcely write for admiring this paper. It reminded me of summer.

But now I waste no time in admiration, but kick off my slippers, wrap myself in a dust sheet and climb on to the bed, which has all its curtains closely drawn. I pull them a little apart on the side by the window, so that light may shine on my notebook, and then, in perfect quietness, like an Arab in his tent, I sit and write until I hear the first gong.

As I write in pencil there can be no danger of spilt ink and I always take care to pull the bed curtains together again and leave the dust sheet exactly as I found it. I have begun a novel.

The cabinet-maker from London works from seven in the morning until eight at night and everything he asks for is left outside the door of the little parlour. And yet he nearly returned to London after the first fortnight.

It seems that he became enraged by Uncle Pescott's endless instructions and the inspections that Uncle Pescott carried out several times a day.

Prue, who polishes the chairs in the corridor outside the little parlour as often as she has a few minutes to spare, came flying up to us with the report of a terrible quarrel between the cabinet-maker and Uncle Pescott.

"They was shoutin' against each other," said Prue, "and

that Mr. Dobson from London were winnin'. Told the Squire he knowed less about joinery than a silly, new apprentice and that he, John Dobson, were a master o' the craft and not a jackass to be gettin' orders from a hignoramus. I never heard tell o' such a animal," said Prue, "but it must be a nasty creature.

"The Squire shouted too, but that Mr. Dobson said he'd work in peace and quiet or not at all, and from the sounds that come out o' the parlour it seemed he were gatherin' up his tools. So then the Squire come climbin' down and promised he'll look at what's bein' done only once a day. And there's our Miss Luce as knows all that's goin' on and never opens her mouth."

"I'm sorry, Prue," I said.

"I've heard what sounds like sawin'," said Prue, "and I've smelled what smells like glue. Maybe it's the satin linin' that's bein' glued in. The smell would turn my stomach but maybe the Squire won't notice—once he's inside. Not but what he's still pretty lively. When he see me in the corridor he almost ran at me. Swore he'd give me a week's notice if I didn't keep away. But I take that wi' a pinch o' salt," said Prue.

"You'd do much better to keep away from both the salt and the corridor, Prue," I said.

Chapter 9

DOLLS IN THE LIBRARY

February 1857

I HAVE NOT TOUCHED MY JOURNAL FOR SOME TIME BECAUSE I have been in difficulties with my novel. It is not progressing very well. I suppose I need more experience of life.

I am sitting on the bed in my writing room, the curtains drawn round me—except on the window side—and the garden is bright with February sunshine. The snowdrops near the old summer-house have been in bloom for a week.

Yesterday I was present at an extraordinary conversation between Miss Alder and Uncle Pescott.

It was half past nine in the morning and I had just begun the history reading that Mamma had set for me, when Uncle Pescott sent for me.

Prue delivered the message.

"And he wants your Mamma's old patch-bag," she said, "and any bits o' stuff that are left from your best summer dresses. You're to take them to the library, Miss Luce."

"Can Uncle Pescott be planning to make a patchwork quilt?" said Flora, and Isabella began to giggle.

"Well, now," said Prue, "I didn't ask him but I did think o' that myself. Maybe he's afraid o' bein' cold in that thing that's bein' made in the parlour. Maybe he'll leave a note sayin' he's to be wrapped up warm before they fastens the lid. What do you think, Miss Luce?"

"I think you let your imagination run away with you, Prue," I said.

"It don't exactly run," said Prue, "but it noses round a bit."

"Miss Alder's gig's coming up the drive," said Harry, who had used the interruption to abandon his sums and stroll to the window.

"Mamma didn't tell us she was coming," said Isabella.

"Perhaps Uncle Pescott sent for her," said George.

"Ah, then the Squire must be wantin' a patchwork weskit," said Prue. "It'll be nice and cheap and that'll please him. You'd better hurry, Miss Luce."

Miss Alder was already in the library when I arrived with the patch-bag. She and Uncle Pescott were talking about the weather. I have observed that Uncle Pescott never immediately speaks of the subject he wishes to discuss but broaches it suddenly as though he wishes to catch his listener unawares.

I said, "Good Morning," and waited.

Miss Alder smiled at me, but Uncle Pescott appeared not to hear and remarked that most of February had been extremely mild.

"But," he added, "my gardeners have been too lazy to make full use of the weather. I was inspecting my rose bushes yesterday and discovered that they were still unpruned. They're idle scoundrels, these villagers, as no doubt you've discovered for yourself, Miss Alder."

"On the contrary," said Miss Alder. "I've a great respect for the villagers. They've taught me much of what I know about the country. I knew nothing when I came from London."

"Indeed," said Uncle Pescott. "Indeed!"

"For a number of years I was regarded as a foreigner," said Miss Alder, "and it wasn't until I bought an old dolls' house, for the village children, and opened a room for them to play

55

in, that Rindle Green accepted me. Your gardeners, by the way, were wise not to prune the roses. There is still a danger of frost at night and cold winds."

"Indeed!" said Uncle Pescott. "It is curious that you have mentioned the old dolls' house, because I have been intending to speak to you about it. I should, in fact, have done so before if I had not been fully occupied with an important project that I have in hand. I must tell you, Miss Alder, that I consider it both ridiculous and unfitting that poor village children should be encouraged to waste their time playing with toys that the parents themselves cannot afford. I understand that the children have free access to this play-room of yours. I must tell you I thoroughly disapprove. The children who are not at school should be working, helping their mothers or earning a few pence in the fields. There is work in the country that even little children can undertake. I must insist that you close the play-room."

I saw Miss Alder begin to draw on her gloves. "I must remind you, Mr. Pescott," she said, "that I live in my own cottage and also possess the small building that is attached to it. The dolls' house and other toys are my property, and the village children, who play with them, are my guests. Good morning!"

She stepped briskly towards the door and would have left the library without another word if Uncle Pescott had not hurried after her.

His face was angry, but it appeared that there was still a great deal he wished to say. "We will not quarrel," he cried. "We will not disagree over so small a matter, Miss Alder. I did not request you to come here with the intention of causing you a moment's distress. There is a more important subject to be discussed. Pray come over to my desk. You too, Lucinda."

Miss Alder seemed to hesitate.

I was still standing near the door holding the patch-bag and she came up .o me and took my hand. Then we both walked

56

over to Uncle Pescott's desk. Lying on it was a collection of tiny, wooden dolls, each with painted hair, black eyes and bright red cheeks.

One was slightly larger than the others. None of them wore any clothes and their small jointed limbs were almost as thin as match-sticks.

"These," said Uncle Pescott, "represent the children and their Mamma."

Miss Alder looked down at the dolls and said nothing.

"As you see," said Uncle Pescott, "They are in need of garments—they must, in fact, be clothed."

"I had observed as much," said Miss Alder.

"That is why I requested your presence," said Uncle Pescott. "I trust you are willing to undertake this small commission."

I saw Miss Alder was struggling to suppress both bewilderment and laughter and looked quickly away for fear I too might be tempted to laugh.

"Surely Lucinda and her sisters are a little old to play with dolls?" said Miss Alder at last. "I'm extremely busy. At this time of year many of my clients order new summer costumes and I've undertaken as much——"

"I see I must be more explicit," said Uncle Pescott. "These dolls, which represent my relatives, are not for the girls to play with. These dolls are to be placed in a dolls' house which is, at this moment, being constructed in the room next door."

"A dolls' house?" said Miss Alder. "And who, pray, is to play with it?"

"No one is to play with it," said Uncle Pescott sharply, "and I beg, Miss Alder, that you will regard what I have told you as a close secret. In due course all will be made public, but I have no desire to disclose my intentions at the moment. Can I rely on you to remain silent?"

"I believe you can rely on my discretion," said Miss Alder.

"Then I must tell you," said Uncle Pescott, "that this will

be no common dolls' house, but an exact model of the Manor. Work on it has progressed so far that I now feel justified in considering the furnishings—which will, as nearly as possible, correspond to the actual furnishings of the Manor—and the dolls which will represent myself and my relatives. I have decided to disregard the servants since they would add considerably to the expense."

"And what is Lucinda doing with the patch-bag?" asked Miss Alder. "And where is your doll, Mr. Pescott?"

Uncle Pescott pushed aside the chair, opened the middle drawer of his desk and took out a small gentleman doll with a tinted wax face and black clothes. It was considerably larger than our wooden dolls although Uncle Pescott himself is a short man.

"I discovered this in London," he said. "And shall order myself new dark clothes so that there shall be no doubt that I am represented in the dolls' house. I intend that the completed dolls' house shall be exhibited on Midsummer Day and shall invite my friends to the Manor to view it. I have hopes that Lord and Lady Elliston and the Honourable Mrs. Billing will honour us with their company."

"And the patch-bag?" said Miss Alder.

"Ah, yes," said Uncle Pescott. "You must understand, Miss Alder, that I wish the wooden dolls to be dressed in exact copies of the clothes my relatives habitually wear to church in summer—their best clothes, in fact. Lucinda, I believe, will be able to provide you with sufficient pieces of the original materials to carry out this idea."

"There are only small snippets left," I said. "Mamma has already used all the larger pieces for repairing our dresses."

"Well, open the bag, Lucinda, and show Miss Alder what you have," said Uncle Pescott.

"There is no need," said Miss Alder. "I must absolutely refuse your commission, Mr. Pescott."

"Refuse!" said Uncle Pescott. "Refuse! And why, pray,

58

should you refuse? There is time enough and I am prepared to pay a reasonable price. I must tell you that I am not used to refusals and cannot accept yours."

"I must repeat it then," said Miss Alder. "I refuse to accept the task of dressing these dolls. I have my reputation to consider."

"Indeed!" said Uncle Pescott. "I should have thought that an order from the Squire of Rindle Green could scarcely diminish the reputation of a village dressmaker."

"I see I must enlighten you then," said Miss Alder. "The clothes the children and their mother are forced to wear are old and unfashionable. I should not care to copy them. The clothes I make are always à la mode."

"Indeed!" said Uncle Pescott.

"You must understand," said Miss Alder, "that my clients

appreciate not only my workmanship, but my knowledge of Fashion itself and its possibilities. Each costume I create is designed for an individual client, and I never repeat it. I may add, Mr. Pescott, that I've a cousin in Paris who sends me reports of all the latest trends, so I'm frequently in possession of the newest French details before London itself hears of them. Lady Elliston has insisted, on more than one occasion, that had I remained in London I could easily have rivalled Madame Elise, with a large and prosperous establishment.

"Lady Elliston, I may say, is one of my most valued clients, and it was, in fact, her mother-in-law, the old Lady Elliston, who introduced me to this part of the country. I now have clients in most of the large mansions that lie within a ten-mile radius of Rindle Green and my reputation for both taste and originality is, I believe, still spreading. So, Mr. Pescott, you will understand why I decline your commission."

It was my turn now to be astonished. I had never before heard Miss Alder talk in this manner and it seemed so strangely unlike her and all I knew of her that I could scarcely believe I had heard correctly.

"I begin to understand you," said Uncle Pescott. "I had no idea that you, Miss Alder, were a kind of local genius and celebrity. I am told nothing, either in this house or the village. Shall we then array the dolls in the latest Paris fashions? Shall we make them miniature models to exhibit your skill? The idea must surely appeal to you? And I am prepared to accept—nay—even to applaud it. What do you say, Miss Alder?"

Miss Alder did not immediately reply and Uncle Pescott repeated, "What do you say?"

"I understand," said Miss Alder at last, "that you intend to invite your friends to inspect the dolls' house, Mr. Pescott. No doubt you will wish the day to be something of a grand occasion, something both unique and memorable. No doubt you will wish your sister-in-law and all the children to attend the celebration so that your guests may meet, at one and the same time, both your relatives and the little dolls that represent them? That, certainly, is your intention, Mr. Pescott."

"I have scarcely yet had time to consider the actual arrangements for the day," said Uncle Pescott, "but the idea is original. Yes, Miss Alder, I believe I shall undoubtedly carry out the suggestion. I should, in all probability, have thought of it myself. Well, then—you accept my commission to dress the dolls?"

"Your sister-in-law and the children will, of course, have to have new costumes to match those of the dolls," said Miss Alder. "It's unthinkable that your relatives, Mr. Pescott, should appear in dresses that are shabby and unfashionable, when the dolls are newly dressed. I take it that we are agreed on that point. Very well then. I accept both commissions."

"But I did not intend——" began Uncle Pescott.

"Of course my present orders must be completed first," said Miss Alder. "Lady Elliston would never forgive me if I failed to deliver her new dresses in time for Easter. But I'll bring a collection of my coloured plates for your sister-in-law to study, Mr. Pescott, and will make a few preliminary——"

"But I did not intend——" said Uncle Pescott.

"Clothes worn in the country should be simple," said Miss Alder, "but simplicity, as I often tell my clients, does not preclude elegance. Now I beg that you'll excuse me, as Lady Elliston is to have a fitting in the early afternoon and I've to drive over to Ramsford. Pray don't bother to ring, Mr. Pescott, Lucinda will see me to the door. Good morning!"

As Uncle Pescott said nothing I followed her out of the library. We paused for a moment in the drive. "I'm afraid I distressed you, Lucinda," she said.

"I didn't know you were so famous, Miss Alder," I said. "You seemed to be someone I didn't recognize."

She gave a kind of sigh. "A dressmaker has sometimes to

61

use more than her needle and thread," she said. "She has to use her knowledge of human nature and her wits."

"Yes," I said.

"My dear, you all very badly need new clothes," said Miss Alder.

Chapter 10

ENCOUNTER IN THE
GREEN BEDROOM

March 1857

MARCH HAS COME AND TODAY IS WARM AND DELIGHTFUL. I
ran up to the orchard this morning before lesson-time and
stood, for a few moments, with my eyes shut and my face
lifted to the sun, and Flora, who had followed me to cut a few
of the small wild daffodils that grow in the orchard grass,
asked me whether I had become a sun-worshipper or was
merely trying to recollect my own name.

Flora has been very amiable lately. Perhaps it is the thought
of her new dress that makes her so good-humoured. We have
all talked about the dresses a great deal—so much, in fact, that I
am becoming a little weary of them as a subject of conversation.
One cannot talk for ever of embroidered muslins, crapes and
tarlatans. But it appears that Flora and Isabella can. They still
have no idea what caused Uncle Pescott's sudden generosity
but know that on Midsummer Day there will be an important
entertainment at the Manor.

Mamma is to have a dress of pale lilac silk, Flora, Isabella
and I will wear white—but our dresses will be differently
made and will have different-coloured sashes—and George
and Harry will have new clothes of light brown.

Prue tells us that Uncle Pescott has been going from room to room, with a notebook, making lists of all the items of furniture. "And what the Squire think he's doin'," said Prue, "I *don't* know. He can't take them tables and sideboards along with him."

I imagine Uncle Pescott is making his lists so that he will know what to buy for the dolls' house. It seems to me quite ridiculous that a grown man should spend his time in this way. I wonder where he will find the tiny pictures, to represent all the new paintings he has bought for the Manor, and where he will find the little marble busts and statuettes and china figures.

I am very unhappy. Uncle Pescott is extremely angry with Mamma and it is my fault.

This is what occurred.

I was sitting, yesterday morning, wrapped in my dust sheet, writing quietly in my writing room, when I heard the key turn in the lock. My key was on the bed beside me and only Uncle Pescott has a second key.

The bed curtains were drawn round me as usual, so I was shut away from the rest of the room, and I sat perfectly still, scarcely daring to breathe. I heard the door close and there was silence for a few seconds and then the sound of footsteps. And I knew it was, indeed, Uncle Pescott, because one of his shoes squeaks.

He seemed to be throwing the dust sheets on the floor and talking to himself. I heard him say, "One mahogany tallboy, one armchair with brass mounts, two chests of drawers, one walnut and gilt mirror!"

Then there was a second silence while, I suppose, he wrote them in his notebook.

(It seems to me now most strange that I never considered that Uncle Pescott might want to catalogue the furniture in the locked bedrooms. Even after Prue had told us he was going from room to room, I still felt safe in my writing room.)

The shoe began to squeak again and seemed to move away while Uncle Pescott continued to murmur to himself.

Then suddenly the footsteps returned.

"One fourposter bed with green brocade curtains," said Uncle Pescott and he was so close that I heard him turn the page of his notebook. "One fourposter bed——" The green curtains were jerked apart and for a single, dreadful minute Uncle Pescott and I stared at each other.

I was too terrified to speak and he, I suppose, was too much astonished.

Then I saw his face become a dark furious red and he closed his notebook and put it in his pocket without taking his eyes off me.

"What are you doing here?" he asked.

"I'm writing," I said.

"Writing?" said Uncle Pescott. "You know you've no business to be here. What are you writing?"

"It's a novel," I said. "And I've taken off my slippers. I've not done any harm, Uncle Pescott."

"Come here," said Uncle Pescott.

I began to wriggle to the edge of the bed, but it was difficult to move quickly because I was so completely wrapped in the dust sheet. Uncle Pescott caught hold of my shoulders and dragged me to the floor.

"Does your mother know you are in here?" he asked.

"No," I said. "Nobody knows."

"Give me the novel," said Uncle Pescott and I handed him the old account book I had been using.

"This will go straight on to the library fire," said Uncle Pescott.

My heart seemed almost to stand still. "No," I cried. "Oh, please, no."

"Rubbish must always be burnt," said Uncle Pescott. "Put on your shoes."

Despair and desperation took hold of me. "It's *my* novel," I shouted, "and you've no right to burn my property. Give it back to me, Uncle Pescott. Give it back to me."

"Put on your shoes," said Uncle Pescott, and he kicked my slippers towards me.

"It's sometimes terrible to be young," I said. "One doesn't know what to do or say. If I went down on my knees, Uncle Pescott, would you give me back my novel?"

"It is going on the fire," said Uncle Pescott. "Put on your shoes."

A kind of fury swept over me. I made as though I would put on my slippers but, instead, flung myself at him, seized his arm and tried to tear the manuscript away from him. But the dust sheet slipped down and tangled about my ankles, and he pushed me away so violently that I fell against the bed.

"Your mother shall hear of this," he said. "You have always been the most undisciplined of all her children. Even your hair is unruly. Your unbridled temper bodes ill for your future. Unless you put on your shoes——"

I did not hear the end of the sentence. I leaned back against the bed and felt tears streaming down my face.

In the end I put on my slippers and Uncle Pescott pushed me out of the room and down the stairs ahead of him.

The library fire was burning quietly, but Uncle Pescott thrust the poker among the logs and made a fierce blaze.

Then he tore my novel apart and dropped it, page by page, into the flames.

He said nothing, and neither did I. And after a little while I shut my eyes. When he had finished he told me I could go and I opened my eyes and saw the hearth covered with flakes of black, burnt paper.

I did not look at him, but went quickly out of the library and up to our bedroom. Mamma came to me there some time later.

She had been with Uncle Pescott. She uttered no word of reproach, but now I do nothing but reproach myself.

Chapter 11

ENCOUNTER UNDER A TREE

I HAVE FOUND A SUMMER WRITING PLACE AT THE EDGE OF THE woods above High Meadow.

The woods are chiefly of old oaks, with occasional thickets of hazel, but where the woodland slope drops steeply to the meadow a great beech tree leans out towards the sun, with its thick, grey roots clutching the ground.

The tree can, of course, be seen from the meadow, but only a mountaineer could climb up to it. It is screened, from the wood, by a thick hazel copse.

I discovered, by chance, that I could reach the tree by pushing through the hazels and I stepped down, from root to root, to look at the new view of the valley and the Manor.

It was only when I turned to climb back into the wood that I observed a perfect armchair, among the beech roots, formed of the roots themselves. I sat down and was at once so comfortable that it seemed that the chair had been constructed for me. I shall go there to write, when the days are warm enough.

I am writing this in Mamma's bedroom, which I may use, Mamma says, as often as I like. But I am glad I have discovered a place of my own.

Recently Uncle Pescott paid another visit to London. He went for a few days and stayed a fortnight. It is curious how the absence of one person can change a house. Immediately Uncle Pescott had been driven away, we felt as though some dark, heavy weight had been lifted. We heard Mamma laugh again, Flora sang as she brushed her hair in the morning and George, who observes everything, but usually says nothing, began to make small, comical jokes.

As for Prue—her imagination took charge of her. "O' course it's the pattern o' them handles the Squire don't like," she said. "Maybe he wanted flyin' angels on them and that Mr. Dobson give him babies with sparrows' wings, like them on the graves in the churchyard. The Squire were always fussy—even when he won't be there to see them. You mark my words, Miss Luce. The Squire's gone to London to find proper gold angels."

After his London visit Uncle Pescott sent for me. There was a collection of dolls' house furniture spread out on his desk. "Nothing cheap here," said Uncle Pescott. "No shoddy pinewood. No penny articles. Everything of the best quality. Look at this copper tea kettle. There are sixteen pieces in it. So there should be—it cost sixpence. You can boil water in it or make soup. Now look at this warming pan. And this little cupboard."

I stood quietly, waiting to be allowed to go. "Of course the cabinet-maker could have constructed models of all the furniture for me," said Uncle Pescott. "But it would have cost a fortune and I told the man I would not consider it. I must make do with what I can buy in the toyshops and from the toymakers themselves."

The little tables and chairs would have delighted a small child, but they looked ridiculous on Uncle Pescott's desk. I suppose he felt compelled to show his purchases to someone and chose me because only Miss Alder and I know about the dolls' house.

"Well," said Uncle Pescott at last. "Since you seem to have lost your tongue you may go. I must tell you though,

68

Lucinda, that I greatly dislike sulky children. I wonder what will become of you."

April 1857

April has come and day after day I slip through the orchard and follow the path that winds up High Meadow to the woods. Then I climb the track between the trees to my hazel grove and step down my root stairs to my armchair. Now I have a secret place of my own I have began to write poems. I have not yet the heart to try to re-write my novel.

A week has passed and I am returning to my journal to report an encounter I had under my beech tree.

Our afternoon lessons with Mamma were over and I had climbed to my armchair to spend an hour writing. Sunlight lay over the fields and I thought as I had so often thought before when I looked down, that the Manor, with its stables and coach-house and other buildings, look like a huge toy set out by a giant in our quiet valley.

I had been struggling with a poem for perhaps twenty minutes, when I heard a loud rustling in the wood and almost at once a man came climbing quickly down the beech roots, past my chair, and stood still, a little below me, staring at the Manor.

He did not observe me because I had shrunk down in my seat. He turned slowly this way and that, as though he were studying different aspects of the scene, and then held up his hands so that they formed a kind of frame to the landscape.

I could see nothing of him but his rough hair, the hollow curve of his cheek, and the back of his dusty coat, but his appearance was so wild that it seemed to me he must be a thief who was planning to rob the Manor and looking for a means of entrance.

I sat still and silent, crouched in my chair, and thought that as soon as the man went away I must run back to the Manor and warn Mamma.

The man remained gazing down at the Manor for a considerable time. Then he turned slowly and looked up and saw me.

I do not know which of us was the more astonished—he, because he had believed himself to be alone, or I because I had expected a villainous swarthy fellow and saw only a very young man with a sharp, white face.

"Good afternoon," he said, and his hand went up to his head as though he had expected to find a hat there and had forgotten he had none.

"Good afternoon," I said and suddenly—perhaps because I was relieved that he was not a dangerous ruffian—I grew angry. "This is *my* place," I said. "Will you please go away."

"Am I trespassing?" asked the man. "I understood that these woods——"

"I found this place," I said. "No one else has ever found it before. Go away."

"But I've found it too," said the man. "I was looking for a clear view of the valley and the house——"

"Well, now you've had a clear view of the valley and the house there's no need for you to remain," I said. "Pray go away. I've had trouble enough to find a place of my own."

"That's something I've never had," he said, and added, "I've spent the last week walking from London. I've never before been in the country, and I'm unused to country ways and manners. But my easel and paints are up in the wood and I should like to paint the house and the valley from here. The prospect's extremely beautiful. Turner would have been glad to paint it."

"The prospect is *my* prospect. And neither you nor Turner may paint it," I said quickly. I had no idea who Turner was but I was growing desperate because my writing time was dwindling away.

70

The man frowned. "I've heard of arrogant landowners," he said, "but never supposed I should encounter one who claimed exclusive rights over the roots of a tree. And, I may add, never in my life have I conversed with a more disagreeable young lady."

I felt my cheeks grow hot with anger, and I stood up quickly and stepped forward. I longed to overwhelm him with furious words: I even longed to push him down the slope—it would have been very satisfactory to watch him rolling over and over down High Meadow and finally bumping against the orchard wall—but I did neither of these things. Instead I burst into tears.

I was aware, for an instant, of the man's concerned and exasperated face and then the torrent of my tears blotted out both him and the view of the valley. I fumbled for my handkerchief, but could not, at first, find it and when I did find it my tears seemed only to flow the faster and I became so angry with myself that I half forgot my anger with him.

But the man quickly forced me to recollect it. "I see," he said, "that young as you are you've already learnt to play the helpless female. Every sweet and docile young lady, who, of course, desires her own way in everything, recognises that tears are more valuable than words or reason. Only the most brutish and insensitive of men dare stand out against tears. As for me—I can't endure them. I shall look for another place where I can paint in peace. Now for heaven's sake, child, dry your eyes. I'll forget I've ever seen this spot. Good afternoon."

I did not see him go. When my sobs finally ceased it appeared that I had won a victory. My writing place was still entirely mine and only the birds broke the country silence. Sunlight still lay over the valley and the smoke from the Manor chimneys still rose up softly into the spring air.

I had had so few victories in my life that I felt I should rejoice. Yet at the back of my mind an uneasiness was growing that could scarcely be called thought.

"There are a thousand other views of the valley," I told myself and repeated it aloud. "A thousand other views."

But the uneasiness remained. Even the satisfaction of being alone in my armchair could not banish my disquiet.

"The man was ill-mannered to choose precisely this spot," I said and seemed suddenly to hear Uncle Pescott's voice saying, "Precisely! Precisely!"

Then I knew why I was so uneasy. I had behaved like Uncle Pescott. Uncle Pescott had driven me out of the empty bedroom, where I was doing no harm. And I have driven the painter away with as little reason.

I hurriedly picked up my poem-book, climbed my staircase and pushed through the hazels into the wood.

There was no sign of the artist. I searched for him for a considerable time and when I found him he was already at work.

He was sitting on a stool in front of his easel and paid no attention to me when I went and stood beside him.

There were charcoal marks on his canvas and a few patches of colour, but I could not see how it could ever become a picture.

"I came to beg your pardon," I said. "You may sit under my tree, if you wish."

"This is *my* place," he said. "Go away! I've had enough trouble to find a place of my own."

He began to paint a dark shape which, I suppose, was a leaning tree trunk, and took no further notice of me.

But I could not go away. I stood watching silently as he put different quick strokes of colour on the white canvas. "Would you like to sit under my tree tomorrow?" I said at last.

He did not answer.

"Or the day after?" I said.

"I should like one thing only," he said and his voice was hard and fierce. "I should like you to go away. I detest being watched when I'm working."

So I turned and went home without saying anything more.

Chapter 12

SPRING MORNING

I COULD NOT SLEEP THAT NIGHT.

Flora and Isabella had been very curious to know why my eyes were red but Mamma had prevented them from tormenting me with questions. But sleep would not come.

In my mind I repeated, over and over again, the conversation under the beech tree and I believe I have never been as much ashamed as I was that night.

I did not blame the painter for refusing to accept my apology because I believed I should have done the same myself.

The next morning I had a headache and could hardly eat my porridge at breakfast, and Mamma said I was to do no lessons but was either to lie down or go out, for a little time, in the fresh air.

I chose to go out. It was a delightful morning, but my mind was so miserably occupied with thoughts of the day before that I hardly noticed the sunlight or the sweet fresh green of the trees. I believe I watched my feet most of the way.

I crossed High Meadow, came to the woodland track and began to climb up among the oaks. I hoped the painter might still be working at his easel, in the place he had found for himself, but he was not there. So I turned back to my hazel coppice. There were primroses and small white anemones everywhere, but they gave me no pleasure and, indeed, I scarcely saw them, because my head still ached and my spirits were sunk in dejection.

I had dared not look in the mirror that morning for fear I had begun to grow like Uncle Pescott.

I began to descend my staircase, still watching my feet, because the steps are of different heights, but before I came to my chair I stood still, from habit, to look at the valley.

Then I felt my heart leap suddenly with relief and joy. A little below my chair the painter sat with his back to me, painting steadily.

So it appeared that he had, after all, forgiven my rudeness.

I stood for an instant, watching, and then, because I dared not stay, began quietly to climb my stairs again.

But I hesitated and glanced down as I reached the bushes because I should have been glad to wish him "Good morning."

He was standing, with his palette and brushes still in his hands, looking up at me.

"Good morning," he said.

"Good morning," I said.

"Am I trespassing?" he said. And I understood that he was permitting me to forget the day before.

"No, you're not trespassing," I said.

"The prospect of the valley's extremely beautiful from here," he said.

"I've always thought so," I said. "I believe even Mr. Turner would be glad to paint it."

"If he were not dead," said the young man and his voice changed as though he were speaking of a friend.

"I didn't know," I said. "We hear so little in the country. We're never allowed to read our Uncle's newspapers. Was Mr. Turner a good painter?"

"He was a god among painters," said the man. "He painted with air and light. I saw him once. He was walking down

Queen Anne Street, where he had a studio. I longed to speak to him, but lacked the courage. That was in 1850, the year before he died, and I was still a schoolboy. So I stood and watched him walk away and never saw him again."

"What was he like?" I asked.

"What does it matter?" said the painter. "He was an ugly, eccentric old man, but he loved light and flung it on to his canvas as though he were master of the sun itself."

"And do you wish to paint like him?" I asked.

"No, no," said the young man. "Only Turner could paint like Turner. I have to discover my own way. I only know that you and I and the whole valley are wrapped in air and light. Not everyone understands that."

"I expect they never think of it," I said. "I was just about to go away. I don't want to disturb you."

"Perhaps you would care to examine my canvas?" he said. "It's little more than a sketch."

So I walked down the steps again and stood in front of his small painting, and, for some reason it made me feel extraordinarily happy, but I could not see that it was a very good likeness of the Manor and the valley. And I believed he had not even counted the Manor windows.

"Well?" he said.

"I should like to look at this on a cold winter evening," I said. "When the fire's smoking and we can't even make toast."

He smiled and I was astonished at the difference it made to his sharp face. It was the first time I had seen him smile.

"Then I've not entirely failed," he said. "D'you think your Uncle would also like to look at it on a winter evening? I understand he collects pictures."

"Uncle Pescott usually buys pictures of dogs and dead animals," I said. "He likes to admire the way the fur and feathers are painted and the way the highlights are touched in. How did you know that he collects pictures?"

76

"I slept last night in the village of Rindle Green," said the painter, and he added, as though it were a kind of miracle, "In a bed, with sheets and blankets and a pillow."

"Don't you usually sleep in a bed?" I asked.

"I've not slept in one since my Mother died and our home was sold to pay the rent and other bills," he said. "My Father died three years ago and Mother ten months later. But one contrives to sleep quite well without a bed. I've a friend who owns some livery-stables and I've often helped him with the horses and been allowed to work and sleep in the loft. Since I've left London, I've slept in barns and haystacks. But last night I was lucky."

"Did you stay at the inn?" I asked.

He laughed. "I've no money for inns," he said. "In fact, I've no money at all. I spent what I had on paints and canvas before I started out and have already had to sell my hat and watch. I walked to the village last night and then, ridiculously, fell down flat in the High Street and a tall fellow called Pryor picked me up, knocked on the nearest door and dropped me at the feet of the village goddess. She nearly blew my head off with her smelling salts, assisted me to an armchair and finally produced a bowl of bread and soup. After that she left me sitting by her kitchen fire and went out and collected my brushes and paints and all my other property which had flown about the High Street. And for that one act of charity I shall be her slave for life."

"But why did you fall down?" I asked.

"I was hungry," said the young man. "I've always believed that I could train myself to eat less and less so that I should have more money for paints, but Miss Alder convinced me I was wrong. Indeed, when I'd fully recovered, she let fly such a hailstorm of rebukes, admonitions and advice at my head that I promised to mend my ways. It seems that once, in London, she knew a painter who died of a consumption brought on by cold and hunger."

77

"She rarely speaks of London," I said. "Was it she who told you about Uncle Pescott's pictures?"

"Yes. And advised me to paint the most impressive view of the Manor, the front façade, but I preferred to come here. She's washing my other shirt and I've promised to return at mid-day. I slept in a two-roomed cottage that seems to belong to her."

"That's the Baby House," I said. "The village has always called it that. 'Baby House' is another name for dolls' house. There's a real dolls' house in the lower room, where the little village children play."

"I noticed it," he said.

"Miss Alder's cottage is called 'Lion Cottage'," I said. "Because there's a lion's head on the knocker."

"I observed that too," he said. "It seems you think your Uncle won't like my painting. Few people do."

"I do," I said.

"But you're a very young lady," he said. "And very young ladies rarely have much pocket-money."

"We never have any," I said, "and Mamma has no money either. How did you know that Uncle Pescott was my uncle?"

"I described you, in the minutest detail, and Miss Alder said, 'That must have been Lucinda.' "

"My name means light!' I said.

"I was aware of that," said the painter, and suddenly he began to laugh. "Here was I, struggling to force the morning light on to my canvas, and a child of light comes stepping down out of the wood, like an angel on a golden staircase. Perhaps it's a good omen. Perhaps I shall sell a painting. As a matter of fact I *must* sell one."

"Uncle Pescott *might* like a picture of the Manor," I said, "if there were the right number of windows and chimneys and if you made the house look extremely elegant. I don't think he'd care whether the sun was shining or not. And I'm not a

78

child of light. Uncle Pescott says I'm the most undisciplined of all Mamma's children. There are five of us."

"You're lucky. I've no brothers or sisters," said the painter and he began to wipe his brushes. "I shall now go and paint the front of the Manor. And I shall count all the windows three times to make sure I put in the right number. You look a little pale—would you like a biscuit? Miss Alder insisted on giving me a packet because she feared I might starve while I was working."

"No thank you," I said. "I had a headache but it's almost gone. Now I must go back to the Manor and prepare my lessons for Mamma."

"My name's Lancelot Green," said the painter. "We may, perhaps, meet again. Good morning!"

Chapter 13

CONVERSATION IN THE DRIVE

IT WAS WHILE I WAS STUDYING THE GENEALOGY OF KING Henry the Seventh that same morning that I recollected how Uncle Pescott had said, "I must look for some artist to re-draw the Family Tree for me."

I glanced round the school-room. Flora, Isabella and George were working quietly and little Harry was counting his fingers and scowling over his sums.

I stood up quickly. "I must go and find Mamma," I said and I hurried out of the room before Flora could reprove or stop me.

I discovered Mamma in the kitchen-garden. "An artist is painting a picture of the Manor," I said, "and he has no money. I don't know if Uncle Pescott will wish to buy the painting, but I've just recollected that he once said he must find an artist to re-draw the Family Tree. I believe Mr. Green may be able to do this. If I fetch him to you will you take him to Uncle Pescott? Miss Alder once knew an artist who died of a consumption, because he was so hungry and cold, and Mr. Green seems only to have two shirts."

"Is Mr. Green a friend of Miss Alder?" asked Mamma.

"No," I said, "but he fainted in the High Street last night and Miss Alder let him sleep in the Baby House."

"Fetch my bonnet and shawl," said Mamma. "Your Uncle

has, on several occasions, mentioned the Family Tree to me·
and I believe he may be glad to employ Mr. Green. We'll
both go and find him."

I had imagined that Mr. Green would be painting just outside the gates at the end of the drive, but I could not see him
anywhere. It was not until we crossed the road and I looked
across the Rindle that I discovered him half hidden at the
edge of a hawthorn thicket in Stony Meadow.

He must have observed us because, when I waved, he stood
up and came uncertainly towards us.

"Why, he's almost a boy," said Mamma.

He hurried to meet us, when he saw we were waiting for
him, and his hand flew up to his head as he crossed the bridge
and I said, "You never remember, Mr. Green, that you've sold
your hat. Mamma, this is the artist I told you of—Mr. Green,
this is my Mamma."

I had never introduced two people before and feared I had
done it clumsily, but Mamma smiled and said she trusted he
found the Manor a pleasant subject.

"The valley itself is my main subject," said Mr. Green,
"and I find it so beautiful that I'm astonished it's not been
invaded by dozens of other painters."

"You're the first we've ever seen," said Mamma. "Our
village is only seven miles from the railway, but we're so
isolated here, at the end of the valley, that we might be a
thousand miles from London."

"Could you draw a Family Tree, Mr. Green?" I asked and
he looked so astonished at the rapid change in the conversation that I had quickly to explain about Uncle Pescott's copy
that had been partly eaten by the London mice.

"Both my grandfather and my father were engravers," he
said, "and I know something of lettering, although I never
wished to be anything but a painter."

"Then will you go with Mamma to Uncle Pescott?" I said.

I saw him hesitate, and Mamma, who is quick to observe

such things, said gently that there was no need for him to make up his mind at once.

"But you could, perhaps, hear what my brother-in-law has to say," she said.

"It'll be quite safe to leave your easel and paints where they are," I said. "There are no cows in this part of the valley."

"I had hoped to sell a painting," he said slowly, "but since that seems a very dubious hope and since one must eat I shall be glad to go with you."

I should have run back to the school-room, when we reached the door of the Manor, if Mamma had not taken my hand and said that I should go with them to the library. "Your Uncle will be pleased that you recollected his wish," she said and there was not time to explain that it was not Uncle Pescott's wish, but Mr. Green's need that had been in my mind.

Uncle Pescott was sitting, as usual, behind his desk.

He said, "Well, to what do I owe this extraordinary interruption?" and then, seeing Mr. Green behind Mamma, "Who is this young man?"

Mamma explained in as few words as possible. "An artist!" said Uncle Pescott. "A painter! Indeed! That's extremely interesting. Have you good eyesight, young man?"

"I believe so," said Mr. Green.

"And you are able to copy anything that is set before you? You have training and experience?"

"I worked at the Academy Schools for two years," said Mr. Green. "Then my Father died and, although the schools were free, I had to find work. I've drawn from the Antique and copied the works of Old Masters."

"But you did not take the full course?" said Uncle Pescott. "You did not complete your studies?"

"The full length of the course used to be ten years, but even when it was reduced to seven years, few students could stay so long," said Mr. Green and he spoke as sharply as Uncle Pescott.

"Indeed!" said Uncle Pescott. "Indeed! I must tell you,

82

young man, that I have no very high opinion of painters. They are often, I believe, wild, feckless and unprincipled. There are a number of established artists, of course, who are well-thought-of and highly respected but you scarcely look——"

"I'm neither established, well-thought-of nor highly respected," said Mr. Green, "because no one has ever heard of me. But I'm still a painter."

"Precisely!" said Uncle Pescott. "And I may, perhaps, be able to make use of you. Yes, yes, I think so."

"And I think *not*," said Mr. Green and turned towards the door.

"I was, of course, speaking of artists in general," said Uncle Pescott. "I believe one should speak one's mind. I had no intention——"

"Good morning," said Mr. Green and he opened the library door and was gone.

A dreadful disappointment took hold of me. I had hoped that, for once, I might prove useful to another human creature, but it seemed that nothing I attempted could succeed.

"I'll go back to my lessons," I said.

"You'll do nothing of the sort," said Uncle Pescott. "You'll fetch that young man back. Tell him I have a great deal of work I should like him to undertake. Tell him——"

"He'll not come back, Uncle Pescott," I said.

"Tell him that I had no wish to offend him and am prepared to be generous," said Uncle Pescott.

"He won't come back," I said.

"Nonsense!" said Uncle Pescott. "He must be made to come back. Tell him that I shall only require him to work for me for part of each day and that I will provide him with a quiet room as a studio. Tell him that I shall allow him to order, from London, anything he needs in the way of materials. Tell him that in his free time he may paint where he likes in the garden or orchard or anywhere in the valley."

"Go and try, my love," said Mamma.

I caught Mr. Green up half-way down the drive. He was striding towards the gate at such a furious pace that I thought I should have to run after him all the way back to his painting place.

But he heard me shouting and waited for me. I began to repeat to him all that Uncle Pescott had said and he stood still, listening and watching me. I had run so fast that I had frequently to pause for breath.

When I had finished, he said, "You've a good memory, Lucinda."

"I know I have," I said.

"Now tell me," he said. "Would you go back?"

"No," I said.

"And do you expect me to?"

"No," I said.

"There's your answer then," said Mr. Green.

"Of course I'm not a painter," I said, "and I've no particular wish to paint the valley. But if I *were* a painter, and if I had discovered a valley that no one else had painted and if I were offered the chance not only of painting that valley but of earning a little money, I believe I might consider——"

"No," said Mr. Green.

"The days are growing longer," I said, "and there will be more and more painting time. On summer mornings there is sometimes a lovely haze over the hills and on summer evenings one walks in a blaze of light, with a curious thin shadow. And there is a scent of honeysuckle in the fields."

"There are enough shadows in London," he said. "Strange! I had almost forgotten London. But one dare not look too closely at some of the shadows in London. There have been times when a begging woman or a crying child has almost forced me to throw away my brushes."

"I hope you'll never do that," I said. "Now I must go back to Uncle Pescott."

"Have you quite recovered your breath?" he asked.

"Yes," I said.

"Very well then," he said and paused for so long that I asked him what I was to say.

"Will you be so kind as to walk slowly back to the house," he said, "and tell your Uncle that I shall remain on this spot for precisely ten minutes by the sun, after you have reached the front door. Tell him that if he wishes to speak to me again he may come out himself and make his proposals. And that if they are courteously worded and as courteously delivered I may be prepared to consider them."

"May I say that in my own way?" I asked.

"In any way you choose," he said, "but without embellishments."

I flew back to the house. The front door was still open and Uncle Pescott was waiting on the steps alone.

It seemed that he had sent Mamma back to her duties and had been watching me.

"Well?" he said. "Well?"

"Mr. Green will remain in the drive for the next ten minutes," I said, "so if you wish to speak to him again——"

"Excellent!" said Uncle Pescott. "Excellent! These hot-headed young men always have second thoughts. No doubt he is thankful now that I was able to preserve a modicum of patience. I will go out at once to him and make my proposals."

"I think he is not at all thankful, Uncle Pescott," I said. "So please——"

"I understand you," said Uncle Pescott. "Yes, yes, one must tread warily with these self-styled geniuses. I will say what I have to say without uttering one word of reproach or displeasure. If his manners leave a good deal to be desired it is, I suspect, because his parents were inferior! Of course you have guessed, Lucinda, what I have in mind for him?"

"You wish him to re-draw the Family Tree," I said.

"No, no," said Uncle Pescott. "That can wait. You must

86

recollect that I once mentioned that the pictures for the dolls' house were a problem. You must also recollect that I stated I should find a solution to that problem when I had had time to give my mind to it. I intend that Mr. Green shall make a small copy of every picture in the Manor, for the dolls' house."

So now Mr. Green works for five hours a day at the Manor, from seven o'clock until nine o'clock in the morning and again from half past nine until half past twelve.

After that he is free to return to his own painting. Uncle Pescott has given him the green bedroom as a studio, and when the clock strikes nine each morning I have to knock at the door and carry in a tray with a large cup of coffee and two slices of bread and butter.

This gives me great pleasure (although I do not believe Uncle Pescott intended it should) because I can examine the miniature pictures and also have a little conversation with Mr. Green.

Every morning before he leaves the Manor, he locks all his paints and fine brushes away so that his work-table is left entirely clear and no one can guess what he is doing. Uncle Pescott insists that this is necessary because Tom and one of the other men have to carry away the paintings that have already been copied and bring up fresh ones to the green bedroom. Mr. Green marks those he no longer needs with a chalk mark and keeps Uncle Pescott's paints and brushes separate from his own.

Mr. Pryor has constructed a rough easel to hold the paintings.

Since Mr. Green's arrival Prue has been in a wonderful state of excitement and conjecture. "O' course you know what it is, Miss Luce," she said. "Them great pictures is bein' cleaned and polished and I'll tell you for why. The Squire's ordered two new suits and that fancy weskit from Miss Alder, and he's goin' up to London with all them pictures because he know he can't take them to the churchyard. He's goin' to give them to the Queen. The Squire'll lay them out on the carpet at Windsor and she'll pat him on the shoulder with her gold sword and then he'll be Lord Pescott, like Lord Elliston, and you and your Mamma will be Ladyships."

"I'm afraid you'll be very much disappointed, Prue," I said.

"I never been disappointed in my life," said Prue. "And don't you laugh, your Ladyship."

Chapter 14

CONVERSATION IN THE
GREEN BEDROOM

April 1857

SEVERAL TIMES A WEEK MISS ALDER DRIVES UP FROM THE VILLAGE in her gig, to fit the new dresses. Flora's is now finished, Isabella's almost finished and Mamma's cut out and partly tacked. Mine is not yet begun.

I enjoy Miss Alder's visits. She usually arrives just after breakfast and stays until we settle to our lessons at half past nine. She leaves her gig in the drive and Thimble, her little horse, stands waiting patiently until she returns to him. Harry rushes downstairs to give him a piece of sugar.

When the fittings are over Miss Alder visits Mr. Green's studio in the green bedroom. He now rents the top room of the Baby House and it seems that Miss Alder is the one person he is always glad to see.

I have grown accustomed to writing "Mr. Green", but he remarked the other morning, when I carried in his coffee, that he would feel more comfortable if I forgot his surname.

"But what shall I call you?" I asked. "Would you like to be called Mr. Lancelot? Or perhaps Mr. Lance?"

"A lance is a sharp, thrusting weapon," he said. "I trust I am neither sharp nor thrusting."

"Your face is less sharp than it was," I said, "because Miss Alder sees that you eat the proper meals. But——"

"But what?" he said. "Am I not amiable, punctual and quiet? Am I not an admirable employee? Could even Squire Pescott find fault with me?"

"But I still don't know what to call you," I said. I should have liked to point out that there were times when he appeared to be anything but amiable, but he was frowning so ferociously that I kept the remark to myself.

"Shall I call you Mr. Lot?" I asked.

"Let it be plain Lot," he said. "That's what Miss Alder calls me."

A few minutes later he opened the door to Miss Alder herself and his frown vanished. I believe he never forgets that she picked up his paints and brushes from the High Street.

"You come like a goddess and are as welcome as one," he said.

"Since goddesses belong to antiquity I take it that your welcome is a respectful comment on my grey hairs," said Miss Alder. "Good morning, Lucinda."

"Your three grey hairs are invisible. And goddesses are immortal," said Lot. "Shall I pour you a libation of coffee or would you prefer to drink it? Lucinda has only just brought it."

"I'd prefer to see you drink it while it's still hot," said Miss Alder. "And don't forget your bread and butter."

"I've just been translated," said Lot. "Mr. Green is no more and I am become Lot."

"Good," said Miss Alder. "But I hope there's no danger that Lucinda will be turned into a pillar of salt when she next appears with your tray." And it seemed to me she spoke a little tartly—I still cannot imagine why.

"No danger whatever," said Lot. "I believe it was Lot's wife who was changed into salt and that was because she looked over her shoulder. As I've no intention of marrying, no beautiful young lady need fear crystallization. Now come and look at this monstrous little masterpiece I've just finished.

The Squire's original is, of course, a fake, but the Squire believes himself to be a connoisseur and wouldn't believe me when I told him so. I believe a large number of fakes are being sold these days. I think my copy's an improvement."

Sometimes Lot has his mid-day meal with us in the schoolroom, and then George and Harry insist on sitting next to him, and he laughs and jokes and tells them such preposterous stories that even Mamma has to smile. But he treats Flora and Isabella with the utmost politeness, and they scarcely say two words to him and criticise him in private with great severity. Flora objects to the paint on his coat, the colour of his hair and the shape of his nose, and Isabella agrees with her in everything and adds that his eyes are too deep-set to be gentlemanly. Flora has grown extremely ladylike since her new dress was finished and Isabella strives to be ladylike too. Fortunately Lot never seems to notice the disapproving glances that are flung at him.

May 1857

It is now several weeks since Lot began his work on the dolls' house pictures. May has come and the orchard is so thick with apple blossom that it appears that some lovely cloud has settled on the slope of the hill. It is wonderful to feel the warmth of the sun and to be no longer cold. In the evening such a sweetness fills the garden that I can scarcely bear to come in to supper.

The cabinet-maker is still shut away in the little parlour, but Uncle Pescott has already sent out the invitations to his Midsummer Day entertainment. He told me this himself. "The expenses have been hugely in excess of anything I imagined," he said. "I have been forced to have a stand, with hidden wheels, constructed so that the dolls' house may be moved smoothly from place to place. I trust Lord and Lady Elliston and the Honourable Mrs. Billing will appreciate all that has been done. The Rectors of Rindle Green and Rindlebridge are bound to be delighted."

Lot has grown more silent lately and yesterday we nearly quarrelled.

I found him staring out of the window instead of working. "I've painted twenty-three of the Squire's pictures for the dolls' house," he said, "Twenty-three! And still more and more are brought to me. Twenty-three tiny, miserable copies of bad paintings.! Twenty-three memorials to my own stupidity! I should never have agreed to the Squire's proposals."

"You needed money," I said.

"Yes, yes. I needed money," said Lot. "But there's not a picture in this house, apart from the old, stiff family portraits, that isn't either a fake or a daub or a cheap imitation of some Old Master. I'm weary of them, Lucinda."

"But you needed money," I said. "One has to have money."

"Squire Pescott comes up here," said Lot, "and prances across the room to look over my shoulder, and says, 'Excellent! Excellent!' and prances out again. And he believes that I'm gratified by his praise, while I despise him for his ignorance and impertinence. But I despise myself more, for my silence. I despise myself infinitely more."

"But you hadn't any money," I said.

"The Squire knows nothing of painting," said Lot. "He knows less than nothing. He has the taste of a poulterer. And he despises me, because I've no banking account, as much as I despise him. But he wants my work and I want a few more of his gold sovereigns. So we both hide our sentiments, we both dissemble. And I'm as bad as he, Lucinda. I should have asked for work on the farm. I'm weary of this whole stupid farce."

"It wasn't a farce. You needed the money," I said. "It's dreadful to have no money. And no more labourers are needed on the farm."

"The Squire surrounds himself by property of every kind," said Lot. "Statues and pictures, mirrors and clocks—he builds a great barricade of them against the world. But he never notices you've a hole in your shoe. Oh yes, I observed it three days ago, Lucinda. When you knelt down to look for the paint brush I'd dropped."

"It's only a house-shoe," I said. "And I've cardboard inside it."

"One cannot deal in both bad and good," said Lot. "My own painting, which is all that is good about me, is being poisoned. When I sit down to work in the valley now I see a dead landscape of paint, without light or air. If I had a soul I should say it was withering at the roots. This green room has become a prison. I shall go to Squire Pescott and ask to be released from the agreement."

I could think of nothing to say.

The bright morning seemed suddenly cold and dark.

"Well?" said Lot. "Well? Surely a prisoner may escape if he can?"

"Your coffee's getting cold," I said and went hurriedly out of the room.

I found Miss Alder alone in the school-room. The others were all out in the garden. She said, "Why, Lucinda, what's happened?"

"Lot's soul is withering at the roots," I said, "and everything is my fault. Everything is always my fault. It was I who persuaded Lot to listen to Uncle Pescott. Now Lot wants to be released from the agreement. He says the green room is a prison."

"The Squire will never release him," said Miss Alder.

"I'm afraid Lot will walk out of the Manor," I said. "I'm afraid he'll go away."

I felt a tear run down my cheek.

"One must honour one's agreements whatever the state of one's soul," said Miss Alder sharply. "I'll go and speak to Lot."

She was gone for perhaps ten minutes. I stood by the table, struggling not to cry, and hoped that Flora and the others would not come in from the garden.

I heard the clock in the corridor strike a quarter past nine and, through the open school-room window Harry's voice beginning a one-sided conversation with Thimble in the drive.

Then Miss Alder returned with Lot behind her. He came and stood beside me.

"Our goddess with the scissor tongue has scalped me, trampled on me and assured me I'm no gentleman," said Lot. "So I've come to beg your pardon."

"Thank you," I said and felt a tear drip off my chin.

"I should not have tried to ease my mind by abusing your relative," said Lot, "but I'd entirely forgotten he was any connection of yours. You're not going to shed more tears, are you?"

"Of course not," I said, and tears poured down my cheeks. It is *terrible* to cry so easily.

"Must you take everything so much to heart?" said Lot. "Find your handkerchief and wipe your eyes. And for heaven's sake stop. What a crybaby you are."

"I can't stop," I mumbled.

"Then I'll fetch my sketch-book," said Lot suddenly. "Don't stop! Go on till I get back. You look like a little gargoyle. I'll make a sketch of you and have you carved in grey stone, if ever I build a cathedral. Don't stop!"

"Leave the child alone," said Miss Alder. But already a remarkable thing had happened. My tears had stopped. I cannot explain this. Perhaps it was indignation that dried them so quickly.

"I will *not* be a gargoyle," I said. "And I will *not* be sketched."

"A pity," said Lot. "It seems I've missed an opportunity. I must remember always to keep my sketch-book in my pocket. Shall I fetch you a glass of water?"

"No thank you," I said, and forced myself to look up. "Are you laughing at me?" I asked.

"I shouldn't dream of doing such a thing," said Lot, "but I've found a way to stop your tears, and am smiling with relief."

94

Chapter 15

POSTSCRIPT TO A LETTER

May 1857

LOT DID NOT ASK UNCLE PESCOTT TO RELEASE HIM FROM THE agreement but is now working all day at the dolls' house paintings so that he may be free of them more quickly.

Some of Lot's copies I find quite delightful, especially those of the few old portraits that were here before Uncle Pescott came.

There is one picture of three red-cheeked, fat little children, with a brown dog and a toy cart full of flowers, that I particularly like. But I've not dared to say so to Lot.

Yesterday I had tea with Miss Alder in her cottage in the High Street. Uncle Pescott sent for Mamma in the morning and told her that he would be driving into the village in the afternoon and could take any one of us who needed a fitting. It was decided I should go because my new dress has now been cut out and my visit would save Miss Alder a journey.

I had no wish to sit in the carriage with Uncle Pescott and drive in state to the village, but I knew it was useless to protest. We set out at three o'clock.

Uncle Pescott seemed in a good humour and was wearing a new coat. "Well, Lucinda," he said. "Well! It appears that I have not laboured in vain. This morning I received a gracious acceptance of my invitation from the Honourable Mrs. Billing. I have only met her twice but she writes most amiably. I have the letter here. She has added a postscript which is, in fact, the reason for my visit to the village. I intend to read the postscript to Miss Alder. She will, I believe, be both flattered and delighted."

Uncle Pescott took a letter from his pocket and unfolded it carefully. "Listen to this," he said. "The Honourable Mrs. Billing writes, 'Doubtless Miss Alder, the Madame Elise of Rindle Green (as Lady Elliston calls her), has also received an invitation. I trust you will present her to me.' "

"I expect Mrs. Billing wishes Miss Alder to make her a dress," I said.

"That remark is both ill-timed and ill-natured," said Uncle Pescott in his most icy voice, and he put the letter back in his pocket. So I dared say nothing more.

The Green is at the entrance to the village and as we approached it I saw the dark, ragged figure of Mrs. Marden standing at the edge of the grass, watching the road. Her bonnet had tumbled back from her face and her basket was some distance away.

As the carriage drew near she sprang forward and spread wide her arms, as though she would stop it, calling out that at last her Sophie had come.

"The woman's mad," said Uncle Pescott angrily. "She should be shut away. Drive on."

The carriage had slowed to a walking pace and Mrs. Marden was hurrying along beside it. "Drive on!" said Uncle Pescott.

I leaned down. "I'm Lucinda, Mrs. Marden," I said, "Not Sophie. I'm very sorry."

I saw her face change. It was as though a candle in a dark window had been blown out. "Ah yes, Miss," she said. "Ah, yes. I see now I was mistaken. My Sophie is pretty as an angel. But you favour her a little," and she turned away.

We drove in silence to Miss Alder's cottage. Miss Alder was in the sewing room (which runs from the front to the back of the cottage), stooping over her long trestle table. She must have seen us, because she showed no surprise when she opened the door. "Pray come in," she said and ushered us into the parlour.

Uncle Pescott put his hat and gloves on a chair and cleared his throat. "Miss Alder," he said, "this is a pleasant occasion. I have come myself to beg that you will honour us with your presence at the Manor on the afternoon of Midsummer Day. It did not seem necessary to me to send you a formal invitation. The proceedings will commence at half past three. I trust you have no other engagement for June 24th."

"None," said Miss Alder.

"There will be refreshments in the garden after the inspecttion of the dolls' house," said Uncle Pescott. "I have not yet decided on all the details but I believe I shall order a rope to be stretched across part of the lawn so that any villagers who choose may view the whole affair, with the Manor servants, from behind the rope. You, of course, will be accommodated with the Honourable Mrs. Billing and my other friends at some little distance from the rope. I intend there shall be rustic chairs and seats for the comfort of my guests. The entertainment, Miss Alder, will be informal and there will be an alfresco quality about my arrangements that will make for ease and pleasure."

"And if it should rain?" said Miss Alder.

"I have considered that," said Uncle Pescott. "If it should rain the entertainment will be held in the library and the villagers will be able to watch from the terrace outside. As they are about in all weathers a little rain will not hurt them. May I assume then, Miss Alder, that you will come?"

"I regard myself as a villager," said Miss Alder briskly. "I accept your invitation, Mr. Pescott, but shall watch the proceedings from behind the rope, or from the terrace, if it rains."

It seemed that, for a moment, Uncle Pescott was quite taken aback but he quickly recollected himself.

97

He even smiled. "Ah, Miss Alder," he said, "you have always been a little eccentric—or shall we say original? But I understand you are a 'personage' and have a position in Rindle Green. You are appreciated and, indeed, admired. You have a reputation, as you yourself informed me, and can do as you choose. Your independence of mind certainly does you great credit and must have proved a considerable asset in your work. One believes in the honesty of those who say precisely what they think. You see I myself speak frankly."

"Indeed you do," said Miss Alder.

"But I have a letter here," said Uncle Pescott, "a letter with a postscript which will, I believe, not only give you satisfaction, but induce you to change your mind. It is from the Honourable Mrs. Billing."

"Ah yes," said Miss Alder.

"Mrs. Billing writes that she hopes I will present you to her," said Uncle Pescott. "She alludes to you as the Madame Elise of Rindle Green."

"Of course," said Miss Alder.

"I trust, then, that you will attend the celebrations as my invited guest," said Uncle Pescott.

Miss Alder smiled. "Since, as you say, I'm both eccentric and independent, I shall attend with the villagers," she said.

Uncle Pescott thrust the letter back into his pocket. His face was red with anger. "I trust you will change your mind when you have fully considered Mrs. Billing's postscript," he said, "and also the difficulty of my position, if you insist on stationing yourself among the villagers and Manor servants. Now I intend to drive to my picture-dealer's at Ramsford. I shall call for Lucinda on my way home. Good afternoon!"

He left without another word.

"The Honourable Mrs. Billing is a most persistent female," said Miss Alder. "For three years she's been trying to induce me to make her clothes. But I'm growing a little tired of fashionable women. Now come and try on your new dress."

Chapter 16

JACOPO

THE SEWING ROOM HAD WINDOWS AT BOTH THE FRONT AND THE back. Besides the long trestle table it was furnished with a tall, standing mirror, a chair, a deep cupboard where dresses and mantles could be hung, several chests of drawers and a number of bonnet stands. A folded screen leaned against the wall.

While Miss Alder was gathering together the pieces of my dress that were spread on the table, I walked to the back window to look out at the garden.

Forget-me-nots still made a haze of blue under the gooseberry bushes, and a number of roses had opened in the hot afternoon sun and their scent came sweetly through the open window.

As I turned to go back to Miss Alder I observed that there was a picture on the wall that I had not seen before. It was a painting of a serious young woman with dark eyes and a large nose. She wore an old-fashioned striped dress with a white collar, and even if I had not known the small pearl brooch that fastened the collar I should have recognized, at once, that the painting was a portrait of Miss Alder when she was still almost a girl.

The painting seemed to me a little hard in outline and childish, but the likeness was so startling that I stood staring at the picture and entirely forgot that Miss Alder was waiting to fit my new dress.

Suddenly I discovered that she was standing behind me. "That was painted in 1827," she said. "I was twenty at the time."

"It's wonderfully like you, Miss Alder," I said. "Who painted it?"

"A young artist called Jacopo Johnson," said Miss Alder. "His mother was a Roman, and had come to London with the English family for whom she had worked in Rome. His father was a Londoner. But both were dead when I first met Jacopo. Now I must fit your frock."

I stood quietly while Miss Alder snipped and pinned. The dress was simple but seemed to me delightfully elegant. For as long as I could remember I had worn only dresses that had belonged to Flora and Isabella, and it was strange to see myself, in the tall mirror, in a dress that was entirely new and fashionable and was being made only for me. I knew precisely how Cinderella must have felt when she first saw herself in her ball dress, and dear Miss Alder, with her small pincushion fastened to her left wrist, seemed like some benevolent fairy.

"Good," she said at last and helped me avoid the pins as I wriggled out of the dress. "Now we'll have tea. Come into the parlour when you're ready."

I put on my old dress and tidied my hair as quickly as I could. Then I walked across the room to examine the portrait of Miss Alder again.

Jacopo Johnson, I thought, was not very talented. I wondered what had become of him. Then Miss Alder called me to come to tea and I hurried into the parlour.

Perhaps she guessed what was in my mind because, as she handed me my cup of tea, she said, "If it had not been for Jacopo I should never have come to Rindle Green."

"Was he a great friend of yours?" I asked.

"I loved him," said Miss Alder, in her matter-of-fact voice, "but he didn't love me. It's an old story, but I've only recently discovered that I can bear to speak of it."

"It must be very sad," I said.

"My mother died when I was thirteen," said Miss Alder. "So I kept house for my father. He was a prosperous draper in the City of London and we lived over the shop. As I grew older it appeared that I had a talent for dressmaking—I didn't discover it myself but old Lady Elliston did. She came into the shop one day to look at some Indian muslins, and took notice of the house-dress I was wearing, which I had designed and made myself. I was in charge of the shop that day because my father was ill."

"And did you make all Lady Elliston's dresses after that?" I asked.

"No," Miss Alder smiled. "I made her a morning cap and then a bonnet of lavender satin. After that I progressed to an evening turban, of rose-coloured gauze, and a velvet spencer. From the spencer I went on to make her a walking-dress for the country and, after that, she had sufficient confidence in me to entrust all her dressmaking to me. She always sent her carriage to fetch me and it was seen so frequently outside our door that the neighbours assured me that my fortune was made. I was happy then, and I had cause to be. I was young and, although I was both plain and a woman, nothing seemed impossible. London itself, in those days, was smaller and seemed a happier place. The railways had not yet come to sweep away the market gardens, the carriage roads and the houses, and to make thousands homeless. And, although the shopping centres were already spreading towards the west, my father and I were still entirely comfortable among our friends in the City.

"I was astonished and delighted to find that I could please Lady Elliston with my dresses and bonnets and I believe I was half-enchanted by the delightful stuffs I worked with—the poplins and fine muslins, the satins and velvets and striped gauzes. And Lady Elliston herself was always kind and generous.

"There was an attic store-room at the top of the house where my father stored the bales of cloth for which there was no room in the shop. A door and an outside wooden staircase led directly from the attic to our yard at the back. My father and I each had a key to the attic door.

One summer morning Jacopo Johnson walked into the shop and asked to be allowed to repaint our shop sign. He had curling black hair, and black eyes and said he had just repainted the prancing horse on the saddler's sign round the corner.

"My father was taken up with a customer, so I said, 'Pray wait', and Jacopo stood looking round as though he found all the rolls of cloth and the boxes of ribbons and lace both curious and amusing. He smiled at me and told me his name before I had asked it and added that he was an artist and only painted shop signs when he needed money. 'I could paint your portrait,' he said, 'and you and the portrait would be so much alike that all your friends would bow to the portrait.' Jacopo never lacked confidence.

"When my father was free he and Jacopo went outside to examine our sign and my father agreed that a fresh coat of paint would improve it. And from that day until about three months later Jacopo worked only for us.

"It appeared that he was a house-painter as well as an artist and was willing to paint stairs and window-frames as well as shop signs and portraits. So, having finished our shop sign, he set to work on the parlour, and then on the shop itself. He seemed entirely happy while he had any kind of paint brush in his hand and he sang arias from the Italian Opera as he worked. Sometimes our customers lingered in the shop to listen to him."

"Where did he live?" I asked.

"We discovered quite soon that he had no permanent

home," said Miss Alder. "We also discovered that he had been an artists' model and had acquired his training (if you can call it that) by listening to artists' talk and studying their work. He had a small talent but believed always that if he could accumulate enough money to work, for six months, as a serious painter in Rome he would be able to prove to the world that he was a master.

"He was twenty-three years old and so full of energy, gaiety and hope that he seemed to brighten the air about him.

"The June, July and August of that year were the happiest months of my whole life. My father approved of Jacopo, because he worked hard and honestly, and Jacopo himself sang his arias and painted the little portrait of me in his spare time, and was so totally unaware of my feelings that he joked with me about the pretty young ladies who sometimes smiled at him in the streets. Most house-painters start work at six o'clock in the morning, but Jacopo liked to start at half past four, so we put a truckle bed for him in the attic and had a third key cut so that he could use the outside staircase and go in and out as he liked.

"And by the end of that August, he had painted and papered almost the whole of our house and shop, inside and out.

"I believe my father would have found still further work for him, but I myself broke the spell of all that summer's happiness. On September 2nd Jacopo came to me with a small package and in it was a ring. It had been, he said, his mother's, and since I had been kind to him, he would like me to have it. It exactly fitted the small finger of my right hand.

"I began to thank him and in my joy, said more than I had intended. And he suddenly understood.

"I shall never forget his startled, concerned face. He went away two days later. There was nothing else he could do. He told my father that now he had a little money, he intended to set out immediately for Rome and would probably tramp through France and Switzerland. He took my hand at the shop door. 'And when I've painted a great number of beautiful pictures,' he said, 'I shall come home and bring them to show you.'

"That was his kindness—he was always kind. He didn't wish me to know that he'd understood."

"And did he come back?" I asked.

Miss Alder was silent for so long that I thought she had forgotten my question.

"Yes, he came back," she said at last. "He came back three winters later. By then, my father had died and I'd become a fashionable dressmaker with my own establishment and regular customers. I'd turned the shop into a work-room and employed five or six girls. But I still used the attic as a store-room. At that time it appeared that everything I undertook proved successful and fortunate. I worked from early morning until late at night, planning, cutting out, fitting my ladies and sewing. I trained my girls and endeavoured to care for them, but my unhappiness had become a part of my life and even their affection meant little to me. I had lost all recollection of what happiness was like.

"Then, one winter night, I discovered I needed something from the attic and took my candle and climbed the inside ladder because it was freezing outside. I remember that there was a nearly-full moon, but the attic windows were so frosted over that one could see only a blur of light through the glass.

"I placed my candle on one of the shelves and was searching for the trimming I needed when I heard coughing in the yard. All my girls had gone home, the housekeeper was in bed, and it was past twelve o'clock, but I was not particularly afraid. More than once, some poor homeless creature from the streets had climbed the outside stairs in the hope of finding shelter for the night. Three of the girls who worked for me had come to me that way.

"I took my candle, unlocked the door and went out on to the small platform at the top of the staircase. It was a bitter night and the frost was rough and glittering on the wooden steps. Someone was hunched on the bottom steps. When I hurried down I saw it was Jacopo. He was very thin and very ill, but he tried to smile. He said, 'I still have my key. It was so cold——' Then he began to cough again. I wrapped my shawl round his shoulders, and tried to help him to his feet, but he could scarcely stand and I wasn't strong enough to support him. So I said, 'Wait. Don't move' and ran for the house-keeper. She was Scottish and nothing ever surprised her. She woke and came with me at once and together we got Jacopo through the kitchen, up the stairs to the parlour and into a chair by the fire. Then while she heated some milk for him I hurried to get the doctor. He was a friend of mine and would come at any time, but I knew, even before he came, that Jacopo would die.

"He had returned from Rome, tramped the streets in all weathers and half-starved for nearly a year. 'They laughed at my paintings in Rome,' he said, 'and I began to long for London, even the smoke and dirt. A man bought all my pictures —not because he admired my beautiful brush-work but because he could use the canvases—and I suppose everything I did is now painted over with views of St. Peter's or of pretty peasant girls. It's of no importance. As soon as I recover, I shall begin to paint again.'

" 'Why didn't you visit me when you reached London?' I asked.

" 'Because I'd no paintings to show you,' said Jacopo. 'But when I've got rid of this ridiculous cough——'

"He died three days later, in my father's room."

Chapter 17

ART AT TEATIME

I SAT STARING AT MY CUP, SO SAD THAT I DARED NOT SPEAK FOR fear I should cry. There is too much sorrow in the world. I thought of poor Mrs. Marden, for ever waiting for her Sophie to come home.

And then I thought of our own dear Mamma, who had moved softly about our rooms, with a white strange face, after Papa had died. He, too, had been out in all weathers.

In those days, we scarcely mentioned Uncle Pescott, who disapproved of us all and especially of Papa, who was his only brother.

Miss Alder touched my arm. "Your tea's getting cold, Lucinda," she said.

I told her I was only thinking. "Did you come to Rindle Green because Jacopo died?" I asked. I knew she would not think me impertinent.

"Yes," said Miss Alder. "I could no longer endure our old house or London. Lady Elliston took charge of me. She said, 'I'm going into the country and you will come with me', and she brought me down to Ramsford, which was far smaller than it is now because the railway hadn't then been built. Lady Elliston was always happier in the country than she was in London, and day after day, although it was winter, we drove out or walked along the roads and lanes and she let me talk until I had purged away the fierceness of my grief. I've often marvelled that she should have been so infinitely patient and benevolent. In the eyes of the world she was a great lady and I merely a successful dressmaker, but I believe she regarded me as some sort of daughter. She had only her one son and had always longed for a girl."

"But when did you come to Rindle Green?" I asked.

"On one of our winter drives, we passed through the village," said Miss Alder, "and I noticed that this cottage and the Baby House were empty and immediately conceived the idea of buying them. They belonged, like most of the cottages in Rindle Green, to Sir James Pescott and, since he was a friend of Lady Elliston's, he was willing that I should have them. I've been here ever since, except for a few brief visits to London."

"And what happened to your dressmaking establishment and the sewing girls?" I asked.

Miss Alder smiled. "The establishment is still mine and the girls, who are girls no longer, still work for me. Several of them married and their daughters sit beside them at the sewing tables. My cousin took charge of the establishment at first after I left London, but when she married and removed to Paris, the eldest of the girls became my deputy. They are all excellent sempstresses and can carry out exactly the wishes of their customers, but they make dresses and bonnets that are less expensive than those I provide for young Lady Elliston and my other clients."

Miss Alder frowned. "As prosperity increases so does the number of fashionable women and would-be-fashionable women," she said. "But to tell you the truth, Lucinda, I'm sometimes weary of Fashion and not only of Fashion, but of all the noble ladies who patronise me and find it so necessary to have a different dress for every occasion. Young Lady Elliston is an exception, and is also my friend.

"Fashion is a hard mistress and my poor ladies spend hours

every day changing from one costume to another. There are morning dresses, house-dresses and promenade dresses, there are carriage dresses and evening dresses, there are ball dresses and opera dresses. . . . And each must be worn with its appropriate cap or bonnet or head-dress. I suspect that most fashionable women have so little to do that they are glad of the excuse that Fashion offers them, to indulge in even the limited activity of changing their clothes. In all likelihood they choose to live for months of every year in London with the express purpose of pursuing a more active life there in the cause of fashion than they do in the country."

Miss Alder took my cup and poured me a second cup of tea. "I believe one day I shall horrify them all," she said. "I shall burn my patterns, throw away my tape-measure and give all my copies of 'La Belle Assemblée' to the village children, so that they can make paper dolls of the fashion engravings. I shall use Thimble and my gig only for shopping in Ramsford and for summer picnics, and I shall spend my time growing vegetables, looking at the leaves on the trees and listening to the birds in the garden."

"But you are always so busy, Miss Alder," I said. "And there are so few leaves in winter. Surely you'll find such a life tedious?"

"It could scarcely be more tedious than the conversation of some of my clients," said Miss Alder, "or duller than the long discussions on whether the undersleeves shall have three or four bouillons, or the flounces be ruched or pinked.

"And when there are no leaves on the trees I shall turn back to books. Fortunately, they keep their leaves all through the year and there is no end to learning. I shall study the science and art of cultivating the soil—I already know something of it—and shall make myself an expert on tillage, pasturage and forestry. Our very lives depend on the soil and turnips are of far greater importance than tucks or trimmings."

She appeared to have regained her normal cheerfulness and

I dared to ask the question I had hesitated to ask before. "Have you grown happy again in Rindle Green, Miss Alder?" I could not bear to think that she might still be unhappy.

"I believe I've never been happy since Jacopo died," she said slowly. "But here I'm contented. And since Lot was deposited on my floor, I've re-discovered a number of small pleasures that I'd forgotten—the pleasure, for instance, of argument and discussion, and the very simple pleasure of cooking for someone other than myself. Since Lot came, I've allowed myself to think of Jacopo. He would never have become even a tolerable painter, but he had an ardent spirit and endless hope.

"Lot is different. Lot groans and despairs because his painting falls short of the beauty he sees in the natural world and because the glory of light eludes him. But one day Lot will find his own way into Turner's kingdom and then Europe will be forced to recognize a new and great talent."

"Lot will go away," I said, "and here, shut in our valley, we shall never know what becomes of him."

And as I said the words, it seemed that a hard cold finger pressed on my heart. Lot was my friend, he had made me cry and he had made me laugh and he had opened a window for me on the huge world outside our valley.

Miss Alder looked at me, smiling. "*You* may not spend the whole of your life in the Rindle Valley," she said.

There was a shout from the High Street and Lot waved as he passed the gate. We heard the front door of the Baby House open and shut, and a few minutes later Lot knocked on the parlour door. Years ago Miss Alder had had a door constructed in the wall, between her work-room and the Baby House, so that, when the little children came to play with the dolls' house, she could leave the door ajar and know that they were safe.

Lot had walked through this door. He said, "Hail to thee, blithe spirit!" and dropped a dog-rose on Miss Alder's plate.

"I came home through the fields," he added. "Good evening Lucinda."

"Good evening," I said.

"How is your soul this evening?" asked Miss Alder.

"Struggling for survival," said Lot. "The days in the green bedroom grow longer and longer, but Squire Pescott was absent this afternoon, so I was not honoured with a visit. That, at least, was a blessing. I've finished another monstrous little still-life of dead birds and a shining, dead fish. Why doesn't your Uncle collect sweet, domestic scenes, Lucinda? Or pictures that point a moral, or tell a pretty story—the ragged little crossing-sweeper, with his broom and clean bare feet, or the rosy-cheeked young lady mourning for her lost love, or her lost canary—it doesn't matter which? Those are what most people collect."

"I believe Uncle Pescott doesn't care for pictures of that kind," I said.

"He's not in the fashion, then," said Lot. "Shall I tell you what happens? When a real, rosy-cheeked young lady—with her Mamma—sees these pictures she says, 'How delightfully sad', and tells her Papa about them. And her Papa says, "Well, my dear, I believe we can afford them both. I dare say our kind neighbour would acquire them if he could, so I'll undertake to purchase them immediately. Doubtless we can find space for them on the dining-room wall, where our neighbour and his good lady will observe them, when they next come to dine, and will conclude, quite correctly, that the affairs of your Papa's firm are not unprosperous. A gentlemen's possessions indicate very clearly, my dear, how far he and his business are successful. Always remember that.'

"And the rosy-cheeked young lady says, 'Yes, Papa, I'll remember.'"

"Is that what really occurs?" I asked.

"I've never actually asked a rosy-cheeked young lady, because I don't know any," said Lot. "But when I tried to make my fortune by teaching drawing in the home of butchers, bakers and candlestick-makers, I saw so many rooms like picture galleries that I drew my own conclusions. They call this an Age of Prosperity and so it is—for some people. And speculators and manufacturers everywhere buy pictures because picture-buying is fashionable and they hope (although they don't mention this to the rosy-cheeked young ladies) that their pictures will increase in value and prove good investments. Perhaps they will. Perhaps these sensible Papas know what they're doing. I only know that the art of Painting is not served——"

"Two of Turner's chief purchasers were a carriage-maker and an oil merchant," said Miss Alder quietly. "Now I'll make another pot of tea."

"No, no," said Lot. "Remain where you are. I need your reassurance. I'm growing so accustomed to smallness in everything that I believe I shall end my days in a black-beetle's hole, designing postage stamps for Her Majesty."

"In all probability you'll end your days in the Rindle Valley," said Miss Alder, "but fortunately your days are unlikely to end for a considerable number of years and you'll have time to see France, Switzerland and Italy first. Are you hungry?"

"Lucinda's Mamma gave me tea," said Lot, "and the proud and beautiful Miss Flora flung a few haughty words at me. I trust you'll never grow into a proud young lady, Lucinda."

"I'm not beautiful," I said.

"You've a lively and intelligent expression," said Lot, "when you manage to overcome your natural melancholy. Of course, your hair is not as golden as Miss Flora's, nor your figure as fine. And Isabella has shoulders that slope more elegantly than yours. You're decidedly too thin and frequently remind me of a young lady wasp. But apart from that——"

"I've always detested black-beetles," I said. "I prefer to be a wasp."

"Of course, wasps can sting," said Lot. "Whereas poor beetles—"

"Lucinda, in her new dress, suggests a white butterfly, rather than a wasp," said Miss Alder. "You'd better have a piece of cake, Lot."

Uncle Pescott called for me at half past six. Miss Alder took me to the door but did not go out to the carriage and Uncle Pescott remained seated in it and merely raised his hat.

Chapter 18

MIDSUMMER MORNING

June 1857

I AM WRITING THIS ON THE MORNING OF MIDSUMMER DAY. FOR A week excitement has been growing in the village, not only because Midsummer Eve is a time of joy and festivity but because Uncle Pescott's invitation to the villagers to attend his entertainment on Midsummer Day has been taken to mean a general holiday.

According to Prue almost all the inhabitants of Rindle Green will be at the Manor this afternoon.

Prue has given us a description of everything that happened in the village last night. In the evening leafy branches were fastened over all the doors in honour of St. John the Baptist, whose festival it was. Then, as soon as it was dark, a great bonfire was lighted on the Green and tar barrels, on the tops of long poles, were set on fire, while Mr. Pryor and the other men sent rockets rushing up into the sky and the little boys let off crackers. There was a great deal of laughter and shouting and I should have loved to be there, but Uncle Pescott forbids us each year to go near the village on Midsummer Eve.

After the bonfire had died down a long chain of villagers, holding hands, danced through the fields to the Manor Farm, where an old cartwheel was set alight and sent rolling down the long lane that leads to the Rindle. The people of the village believe that if the wheel is still flaming when it reaches the water, the sun will retain some of its strength to the year's end, but that if the wheel rolls into the ditch or is extinguished, there will be miserable, cold days in the near future.

"It run clear down the middle o' the lane," said Prue, "but then, o' course, there weren't nothing else it could do seein' the boys had swep' every stick and stone out o' the way, and hit it wi' bits o' branches to keep it goin'."

The wheel was still burning furiously when it toppled into the water, so now, Prue says, we shall have a very hot, fine summer. I hope so.

It was a warm night and today is cloudless and brilliant. Uncle Pescott's arrangements are complete, the old summerhouse is hung with garlands of artificial roses—which seems ridiculous when real roses are growing on the bushes—and the rope to divide the lawn is already in place.

Uncle Pescott himself has been in a fever of irritation all the week, forever sending for Mamma, overwhelming her with instructions and then sending for her again to countermand them.

But now he is assured of a fine day, he appears calmer. He ordered us all to come to the library immediately after breakfast and smilingly showed us a strange, large shape covered with a dust sheet.

"This," he said, "is the fruit of my thought and labour for the last six months: this is the reason for the gathering of our friends which will take place this afternoon. Lord and Lady Elliston will not, unfortunately, be amongst us, as they are forced to be in London, but their refusal of my invitation was couched in terms which indicated their regret.

"The Honourable Mrs. Billing will be present. Now it is necessary that you should prepare yourselves for the part you are to play in the presentation of this tribute to our forbears and the Manor."

I heard a stifled giggle from Isabella, who was standing behind me, and observed that George had grown red in the face and was staring at his boots.

"Perhaps, Mr. Pescott, you will allow us to see what it is you've spent so much time and thought on," said Mamma, quickly.

"All in good time," said Uncle Pescott. "I must first explain that this tribute will, this afternoon, be set in position on that part of the lawn immediately facing the steps that lead up from the terrace. And I intend to request the Honourable Mrs. Billing to remove the covering. After she has performed that little ceremony, you children will be requested to meet and entertain the guests for the next ten minutes or so. It is essential that you should all know precisely what I expect of you. Very well! I will no longer keep you in suspense."

Uncle Pescott stepped forward and carefully drew off the dust sheet. And there was the dolls' house.

We were all entirely silent.

I believe Mamma and the others were so much astonished they could think of nothing to say, while I, who had known what to expect, was lost in unwilling admiration.

Here was the Manor, its walls and chimneys, its two urns and wide front steps in perfect miniature. Curtains showed at the windows and a tuft of cottonwool smoke rose from the kitchen chimney.

"I'd not expected anything like this," said Mamma, hesitantly, "but it's excellently constructed."

"Any connoisseur would recognise it at once as a masterpiece," said Uncle Pescott. "The interior is as perfect as the exterior. Both back and front are hinged and will open in sections."

He swung back the four sections of the front and there were the wide entrance hall, and the staircase, tiny and exact, rising from floor to floor; there were the two parlours and the drawing-room with its minute, polished pianoforte. Above we

115

could see the school-room and front bedrooms and the passage that led to the five unused bedrooms at the back. And above the bedrooms were the attics and servants' rooms.

The housekeeper's room, the servants' hall and the kitchen, sculleries and pantries were all in the basement and were stocked with kettles and saucepans, crockery and cutlery, brooms and brushes. And throughout the whole dolls' house, every item of furniture had been placed in exactly the position it occupied in the Manor itself.

All the curtains and tablecloths were of the correct colours and most of the walls had been papered with pieces of the same wall papers that had been used in the Manor rooms. (Uncle Pescott always ordered a little extra wallpaper in case patching should be necessary.) In the dolls' house the gilded trellis patterns and stripes looked huge but not out of place and the posies in the green bedroom were indicated by tiny spots of colour. I noticed this when Uncle Pescott opened the back of the dolls' house.

But Lot's little pictures were the most delightful things in the dolls' house. The cabinet-maker had mounted and framed them, in tiny frames of gilded wood, and each hung in its proper position. Even Flora seemed impressed.

"Their very smallness gives them a kind of charm," said Mamma.

"Are you going to play with the dolls' house yourself, Uncle Pescott?" asked Harry.

"It was not constructed for play," said Uncle Pescott stiffly. "It will remain here in the library, and I intend that Lucinda shall dust it and its contents every week."

I understood then that I was still to be punished for my disapproval of the dolls' house at the beginning.

"But now to work," cried Uncle Pescott. "You will all have observed that the dolls' house has no inhabitants. It was essential that I, as master of the Manor, should be represented and since you are all my relatives, I have done you the honour of having Miss Alder dress a small doll to represent each one of you."

He opened the drawer of his desk and took out the gentleman doll and the wooden dolls that I had seen before. But now each one of them was clothed in a perfect copy of the dress each one of us will wear, for the first time, this afternoon. He handed us our dolls and gave Flora Mamma's doll as well.

"I have planned," he said, "that as soon as the Honourable Mrs. Billing has unveiled the dolls' house and all the other guests have had time to examine and admire it, I shall place myself at the top of the steps and wave my handkerchief. And you five children will move, one by one, from the library, each holding, in your right hand, the doll that represents you. You will cross the terrace, climb the steps to the lawn, curtsy to the visitors and then walk towards them, lifting up the doll so that all may see it. You will then place it on a chair in the drawing-room of the dolls' house and withdraw to one side. Flora, you will head the procession and will carry both your own doll and that of your Mamma, since she will be assisting me to entertain our friends. Now I shall go up on the lawn and you will rehearse what you have to do."

We practised walking, curtsying and exhibiting our dolls for more than an hour. Uncle Pescott was very difficult to please. Flora was too slow and Isabella's curtsy was not deep enough. George and Harry bowed too briskly and were reproved for their eagerness to get the business over, and I was sent back again and again because I did not smile.

"Your smiles are of the greatest importance," said Uncle Pescott. "Our guests must see that you delight in the occasion and are happy to present your dolls to them."

"We might as well be dolls ourselves," whispered Flora. "How childish it all is! How extremely stupid!"

"Uncle Pescott should have been a Punch and Judy man,"

said George. "He'd have enjoyed making Judy wag her head. I wish I were Dog Toby. I should like to trot up quietly and bite his ankles."

"But that would be unkind," said Harry.

Chapter 19

THE ENTERTAINMENT

UNCLE PESCOTT'S ENTERTAINMENT IS OVER.

Although I had little expectation of pleasure, I discovered that there is a kind of excitement in wearing a new dress for the first time and, when I saw myself in the large mirror in Mamma's room, I was glad that my full white skirt and turquoise ribbons in no way suggested a young lady wasp.

I had not seen Lot for nearly a week. Since he had finished Uncle Pescott's little pictures he had not been near the Manor, but I knew he was still at the Baby House and hoped he would come to the fête with Miss Alder and the other villagers.

We were all ready so early that after Mamma had gone downstairs, we gathered at the school-room windows to watch the carriages arrive. The villagers had been instructed to use the back entrance. I suppose Uncle Pescott was afraid that their presence in the drive might disconcert the Honourable Mrs. Billing and the other ladies and gentlemen. The Rector of Rindlebridge arrived first with his fat wife, and thin daughter. A young gentleman rode beside their carriage, on a piebald horse, and must have observed us at the windows because he glanced up smiling and raised his hat.

"That's the Rector's son, back from Switzerland," said George. "He's going to teach in the Grammar School at Ramsford. Prue told me. He has red hair, just like his Papa."

"And no doubt he has freckles just like his Papa, too," said Isabella and glanced at Flora to see if she were smiling. But Flora was leaning forward, watching as the young gentleman opened the carriage door for his mother.

"Freckles, on a man, are not necessarily unbecoming," she said, sharply.

Then Uncle Pescott hurried down the front steps to greet his guests and we drew back for fear he should see us.

When we looked out again several carriages were drawn up in the drive and others were approaching. We recognised the doctor of Rindle Green, in his gig, and the curate of Reyne on his black mare. Then an open barouche, with four horses and two footmen, swept up the drive and we caught a glimpse of a plump lady under a purple parasol. Her huge flounced skirt seemed to fill the whole carriage and she looked like a stout pigeon sitting in a nest of yellow silk.

"The Honourable Mrs. Billing has arrived," said Flora, "and there is Uncle Pescott rushing to welcome her. See how eagerly he's helping her to alight! It's a pity she's so fat and so tall. Poor Uncle Pescott will have to spend the rest of the afternoon on tip toe."

Mamma was conducting the other ladies into the house.

"We'll slip down to the library as soon as the drive is empty," said Flora. We had been instructed not to show ourselves until the moment when each one of us stepped out on to the terrace.

As soon as it appeared that all the guests had arrived we crept down to the library and stationed ourselves behind the curtains. Only Flora watched for Uncle Pescott's signal. We could hear conversation and laughter and a continuous murmur that was, I suppose, the villagers of Rindle Green talking among themselves behind the rope.

Suddenly, there was a short silence. "Of all the unendurable things in this world, curiosity is the worst," cried a loud, affected voice. "I, for one, can never endure it." It was a hot still afternoon, and we heard every word.

"The Honourable Mrs. Billing is growing impatient," said Flora.

We heard Uncle Pescott clear his throat.

"If you will do us the honour of raising the veil, your curiosity, my dear Mrs. Billing, will immediately be satisfied," he said.

"Let me, then, disclose the mystery," cried Mrs. Billing, and I imagined her stepping forward, with a great rustling of silk, and drawing the dust sheet off the dolls' house.

"I wonder how long we shall have to wait," said Flora. Her cheeks were flushed and she looked quite beautiful in her new dress.

There was a burst of clapping and then voices crying, "How delightful!" "How original!" "What exquisite workmanship!"

"I, for one, am quite enchanted," said Mrs. Billing and Uncle Pescott answered, "I am more than gratified by your approbation, Mrs. Billing."

"But my dear sir, are we not to see the interior of the dolls' house?" asked one of the gentlemen.

"Of course, of course," said Uncle Pescott. "The whole edifice shall at once be opened for inspection, if you will all be kind enough to stand back for a moment."

It seemed that Uncle Pescott opened both the front and the back of the dolls' house, because there was another burst of clapping and then more exclamations of surprise and admiration.

"The rooms, surely, are exactly as they are in the Manor itself!"

"Observe the library and the wide fireplace!"

"But the pictures—do, pray, look at the pictures!"

"They are real paintings!"

"They are quite astonishing!"

"As exquisite as miniatures!"

"I recollect the picture of the three children over the

drawing-room mantelpiece. I particularly observed it. The expressions are quite perfect."

"And so sweetly pretty! And the toy cart, with the flowers—so wonderfully copied!"

"My dear sir, the pictures are, assuredly, the most extra-ordinary part of your entire conception," said the gentleman who had spoken before. "Where did you discover a painter capable of such work?"

"I, for one, shall insist that the artist be presented to me," cried Mrs. Billing. "Some painters, I believe, are not altogether worthy of attention, but Art can ennoble those who practise it. Where *is* the artist? He should be here."

"I trust I may be able to present him to you a little later," said Uncle Pescott hurriedly, and I guessed that he had not thought it necessary to invite Lot.

"Now," said Uncle Pescott, "you will have noticed that the dolls' house has no residents, except this wax gentleman who represents myself. But if I wave my handkerchief——"

"At last," said Flora and stepped out into the sunshine with a doll in each hand. We edged forward to watch. We saw her mount the steps to the lawn and then the conversation died away and there was a kind of hush.

"Allow me to present my eldest niece, Flora," said Uncle Pescott, loudly. "As you see, she has brought——"

But his words were lost in a great hum of voices, in which I could catch only one clear sentence.

"Such a beautiful young creature!"

Flora must have played her part well, because Uncle Pescott was smiling when he waved his handkerchief the second time.

"It may, perhaps, be a little unorthodox to bring forward children who are not yet out of the school-room," he cried, "but since we are in the country and this is an alfresco gather-ing——"

"Wish me luck," said Isabella and hurried out on to the terrace. When my turn came I was trembling. The terrace appeared enormously wide and the steps enormously high. But as I stepped on to the hot paving stones a sheet of paper fluttered to my feet. I stooped quickly and picked it up. Luckily Uncle Pescott had turned back to his guests. On the paper was a small drawing of a wasp wearing a dress and elegant sash and underneath was written "With compliments to a lovely young lady wasp". But the word "wasp" had been crossed out.

I turned for an instant, and looked up, and a hand waved from the window of the green bedroom. Suddenly I was happy. For the first time in my life I felt confident and unafraid. I tucked the drawing into my sash, walked up the steps and executed my curtsy without haste or agitation. Then I stepped forward and held up my ridiculous little doll so that everyone might see it.

All the ladies and gentlemen were gathered about the dolls' house in a wide semicircle, with Uncle Pescott and Mrs. Billing in front. Mamma stood to one side, with Isabella, but Flora was talking to the thin daughter of the Rector of Rindlebridge, while the red-haired brother stood quietly watching.

Having completed my performance, I placed my doll in the dolls' house.

"Such well-trained girls," said Mrs. Billing. "I, for one, have always believed that children should be rigorously disciplined, but rewarded for good behaviour. I imagine, Mr. Pescott, that each of your charming nieces owns the doll that represents her. There is a kind of appropriateness in the idea."

"Indeed there is," cried Uncle Pescott, "although I had not precisely formulated the thought until you, Mrs. Billing, put it into words. From this moment each of my nieces is the possessor of her doll. But I must not forget my nephews, who have still to be presented."

When George and Harry had performed their parts, which they did very rapidly, the guests settled themselves on the rustic chairs and seats that had been set out for them, and afternoon tea was served.

BARBARA C. FREEMAN.

Flora, Isabella and I were kept so busy handing round plates of sandwiches and little cakes that I had no time to run and speak to Miss Alder or slip up to the green bedroom to see what Lot was doing.

Groups of villagers still stood behind the rope but many had already gone home. I imagine they could have seen almost nothing but the backs of Uncle Pescott's guests and I was ashamed that no refeshment had been offered them after their hot walk.

Flora, I noticed, was especially attentive to the Rector of Rindlebridge's wife and daughter, but once she stood still on the steps, with a cake plate in her hands, staring at nothing and smiling as though she were lost in some curious and pleasant dream.

"It appears that Flora is thinking of the gentleman with two carriages," whispered George, as he passed me.

"The gentleman has only a piebald horse," I said.

Chapter 20

MRS. BILLING

THE HONOURABLE MRS. BILLING TALKED ALL THROUGH TEA.

"I, for one," she said, "am delighted with everything, Mr. Pescott. But you still have not presented Miss Alder to me and I have yet to meet the genius who painted the dolls' house pictures. I have seen other dolls' houses, Mr. Pescott, that could be said to rival yours, but the little paintings are, I believe, unique. I, for one, am quite longing to make the acquaintance of the artist. Pray find him and bring him to me. And perhaps one of your charming nieces could discover Miss Alder. I have hopes of persuading her to undertake an important commission for me—in fact, a ball dress."

"Lucinda shall fetch Miss Alder," said Uncle Pescott. "I believe she is not far away. Hurry, Lucinda!"

"And the genius!" said Mrs. Billing. "He must be told that I, for one, have plans for him."

Miss Alder had already gone home.

"She were a bit put out," said Prue, who came up with a tray of empty cups. "There weren't so much as a mug o' beer or a drop o' tea for anyone, nor a biscuit for the children. It were all a bit of a disappointment. I were quite took by surprise, Miss Luce. Who'd ha' thought the Squire 'ud want to play with a Baby House at his age? There were I, thinkin' he were gettin' ready for the next world and there were he, buyin' all them little chairs and tables. I see them all when I come out with the tea urn. O' course, they do say that some has a second childhood before they're put in the ground. You look a picture, Miss Luce, in that new dress o' yours."

I did not return to Uncle Pescott, but ran to the green bedroom. The dust sheets were all back in their places and it was dark and cool. I believed that only I knew that Lot was there and it seemed to me that if I could persuade him to come with me to Mrs. Billing, Uncle Pescott might be saved from his embarrassment.

Lot was sitting, half-hidden by the climbing roses, beside the open window, with his sketch-book on his knee. He was drawing furiously.

"You played your part charmingly, Lucinda," he said, without looking up. "This room is like a box at the theatre. Look!"

He flicked over the pages of his sketch-book and there was group after group of small figures—gathered round the dolls' house, talking, drinking tea. Some were in bright sunlight, others in the shade of the summer-house, but Lot had seen all of them—the ladies in their wide, flounced skirts and the gentlemen in their more sober clothes—as patterns of light and dark.

"Figures in the open air," said Lot. "You may recognise Mrs. Billing by the size of her crinoline. I could have drawn a whole gallery of portraits, but decided that that would be ungentlemanly since only you knew I was here. I walked up with Miss Alder to return the key of this room, which I forgot to give to your Uncle the other day. I thought I'd leave it on the table here. But the show was so engrossing I couldn't bring myself to leave. I hoped you'd bring me a cup of tea and a half-penny bun."

"I'm afraid I've only brought you a message," I said. "Mrs. Billing wishes to see you. She admires your little paintings and says she has plans for you."

"I make my own plans," said Lot. "Pray tell her so."

"Mrs. Billing wished to see Miss Alder, but she's gone

home," I said. "Don't you understand, Lot, that Uncle Pescott will look ridiculous if he can't present either Miss Alder or you?"

"Nothing can make him look more ridiculous than he is," muttered Lot.

"But I shall be blamed," I said.

"And then, of course, you'll burst into tears," said Lot.

"Yes," I said. "I usually do. It's a great nuisance."

"Very well," said Lot. "Let me be presented to this honourable and enthusiastic lady."

He closed his sketch-book and stood up. "But you must understand, Lucinda, that I can't answer for the consequences."

As Uncle Pescott saw us approaching his anxious expression changed to one of relief, and he smiled and came forward with his hand outstretched. "My dear fellow," he said. "I have just been explaining to Mrs. Billing how your talent struck me immediately. She wishes me to present you to her and, indeed, nothing could gratify me more. My dear Mrs. Billing, here, at last, is our young Michelangelo."

"Ah, young man," cried Mrs. Billing. "You are *more* than talented. I, for one, recognise that you have genius. Your small pictures have astonished and quite overwhelmed me. I have always been easily overwhelmed by fine works of art and your——"

"They are merely copies, Madam," said Lot.

"Yes, yes," said Mrs. Billing, "but there is something about a very small painting that satisfies one's sense of the beautiful, something, in short, that is not possessed by the coarse original. I take it that your labours at the Manor are quite at an end."

"Not quite," said Uncle Pescott quickly. "Not quite, Mrs. Billing. There is still my Family Tree to be re-drawn."

"I've fulfilled all my commitments here," said Lot, "and now I intend to——"

"Intend nothing, young man," cried Mrs. Billing. "Intend nothing. I have made plans for you—plans that will, I am convinced, meet with your perfect approbation. I have a gardener's cottage that will be put at your disposal and you will come to me. I have a huge collection of family portraits that are old and dark and depress me beyond measure, and you will make small copies of all these paintings. You will copy them, in brighter, clearer colours, to hang in my London drawing-room. I entertain a great deal in London. Your reputation will be established."

"I told you, Madam, that I'd already made my plans," said Lot.

"Then you must change them," said Mrs. Billing. "Change them, my dear young man. A monthly salary will be paid to you and your meals——"

"I regret that I must refuse," said Lot.

"I, for one, never accept a refusal," said Mrs. Billing. "Your genius delights me, and we will not quarrel over your remuneration. You will come to me and——"

"No," said Lot. And I saw that he was frowning. Uncle Pescott was making signs to Lot but he paid no attention to them. Mrs. Billing had pursed up her mouth and her voice had grown a little shrill.

"I am sensitive to beauty," she said, "and my mind's made up. I, for one, am never shaken by refusals. I have always had considerable strength of mind. You should understand that, young man. You should also understand that my natural benevolence would never tolerate the waste of such a talent as yours. You will come to me next week. You will copy my pictures."

Suddenly Lot laughed. "Obstinacy may be called 'strength of mind', Madam," he said, "and impertinence may be called 'benevolence', but they remain obstinacy and impertinence. I refuse your offer."

Uncle Pescott had stepped forward as though to intervene, but it appeared that Mrs. Billing had not heard a word and was still thinking of nothing but her plan.

(I believe she must be an extremely stupid lady.)

"And if I am prepared to wait?" she cried. "If I allow you to carry out the other arrangements first. For how long, young man? For how long?"

Lot bowed and I understood that he was very angry. "For at least sixty years, Madam. Good afternoon," he said and walked away.

Chapter 21

THE FLAT PACKAGE

August 1857

LOT HAS GONE. HE WOULD HAVE STAYED ALL THE SUMMER painting in the woods and fields of the Rindle Valley, if it had not been for the Honourable Mrs. Billing.

It appears that immediately after Uncle Pescott's entertainment, she enquired in the village where Lot was staying and, discovering that he rented the top room of the Baby House, she came to the conclusion that Miss Alder (who had already refused to make her dresses and had a reputation for independence) was the cause of Lot's refusal.

I suppose Mrs. Billing's self-esteem is so great that she could find no other explanation.

Two days after the fête she had a note delivered to Miss Alder. Miss Alder's influence was mentioned, in flattering terms, and she was requested to use it to persuade Lot to agree to the plans that Mrs. Billing had made for him.

Miss Alder did not reply.

From then on note followed note.

Mrs. Billing pleaded, commanded, and threatened. Miss Alder dropped the notes into her kitchen fire and did not, at first, even tell Lot she had received them. But Lot was in his room, when, one evening, Mrs. Billing herself called on Miss Alder.

The great barouche, with the four horses, swept down the High Street and stopped outside Miss Alder's cottage, and a tall young footman leapt down and began to hammer on the door. Lot had gone to the window to see what was happening and observed Mrs. Billing sitting haughtily in the carriage under her sunshade.

He had no idea why she had come. Miss Alder did not open the door and eventually the barouche was driven away with the Honourable Mrs. Billing still sitting, like a stout pigeon, in her nest of flounces.

It was only after this visit that Miss Alder told Lot about the notes. She laughed about them and he laughed with her, and repeated the whole ridiculous story to me when he next passed my beech tree on his way to a new painting place.

But after several weeks Mrs. Billing's behaviour ceased to be amusing. At any time of the day her barouche might appear in Rindle Green and the four great horses, clattering down the quiet High Street, would send the small children running for safety.

Usually so little traffic passes through the village that the children who are not at school can play in the streets.

The villagers grew to detest Mrs. Billing. "O' course she's a lady," said Prue, "but not *all* ladies is what you might call 'a lady'. And them great tall footmen behaves like they was dukes of England. It's lucky for them there aren't no mud about this hot weather or the boys 'ud see them white silk legs of theirs didn't stay white for long."

There seemed no reason why Mrs. Billing's visits should ever end. Lot wrote and repeated his refusal and begged Mrs. Billing to accept his decision, but his brief letter seemed only to stir her to further efforts.

She called twice the following day. "She has so little to do and so little to think of that I suppose she's glad of anything to fill her time," said Miss Alder. "But I wish she'd stay away from Rindle Green."

And now Lot has gone.

I was sitting in my armchair, under the beech tree, about a fortnight ago, when he came stepping down the root stairs and stood for a moment looking at the valley.

He had a flat package under his arm and I supposed that, as usual, he had left his easel and stool up in the woods.

I was glad to see him. But when he turned I saw he was frowning. "I'm running away, Lucinda," he said. "I'm returning to London tomorrow. I shall catch the first train from Ramsford in the morning."

"I thought you'd stay until the Autumn," I said, and sat quite still because a dreadful pain had touched my heart.

"I'd planned to stay," said Lot. "But Miss Alder has been pestered long enough. She's begun to listen for the barouche— she listens all day. She's afraid for the village children, and so am I. She's always running out to see they're not in the road and the smallest sound startles her."

"How soon will you come back?" I asked. I endeavoured to speak calmly.

"I don't know. I shan't remain in London," said Lot. "I shall go to France. There are great painters at work there and now that I've a little money——"

"But France is a long way off," I said. "It's across the sea."

"I believe large numbers of people cross the sea and return in perfect safety," said Lot, smiling. "The Honourable Mrs. Billing will be informed that I've gone and Rindle Green will then, I hope, be left in peace."

"Yes," I said. "We shall all be left in peace, for ever and ever. We've no money, so we can't get away. Flora may escape, on a piebald horse, but the rest of us will remain—while Uncle Pescott grows angrier and angrier and Mamma fades into a kind of ghost. And whatever I do or say will always be wrong, but I shall go on dusting the dolls' house week after week, month after month, and year after year."

I am ashamed now that I spoke so wildly. "And how will you

talk to the French people?" I cried. "How will you buy paints and food and get your boots mended?"

My voice sounded cold and fierce, but I was so wrapped in desolation that I hardly knew or cared what I said.

"I shall go first to Miss Alder's cousin in Paris," said Lot.

"Did Miss Alder suggest that you should go to Paris?" I asked.

Lot shook his head. "No, I made up my mind and then consulted her. You know, I'm no longer a little boy, Lucinda. Miss Alder tried to dissuade me at first because of some other painter she'd known."

"That was poor Jacopo," I said. "He's dead."

"Yes," said Lot, "but I shall *not* die. I shall come back and paint the Rindle Valley. Until then here's something for you to look at on winter evenings, when the fire smokes and you can't even make toast."

He stooped and laid the package on my lap. I believe I looked away from him. He seemed already to be gone. "Goodbye," I said.

"Goodbye," said Lot.

When, much later, I opened the parcel I found the view of the Manor and the valley that he had painted under my beech tree. The picture was already framed.

I cannot bear to hang it up. I showed it to Mamma and then put it away in the drawer under my petticoats.

On the day Lot went away Miss Alder called for me at the Manor, in her gig, and drove me to her cottage for tea.

It was very hot. The flaming cartwheel that rolled into the Rindle on Midsummer Eve seems truly to have indicated our blazing summer. I borrowed a volume of poems, by Alfred Tennyson, from Miss Alder and she drove me home about eight o'clock. We talked of Lot. She says she will miss him very much.

We passed poor Mrs. Marden on our way back to the Manor. She had a basket of wet clothes under her arm and had been washing them in the Rindle. Miss Alder says the villagers leave soap for her to find. She is always very clean and respectable. Yet all her clothes are in rags.

Miss Alder stopped the gig and asked if she could drive her to the Manor gates, where the road ends, but Mrs. Marden paid no attention to her and stood silently staring up at me.

"I'm only Lucinda, Mrs. Marden," I said quickly.

"So I see, Miss," she said. "I took you for my Sophie. But it's no great matter—I expect her any day now."

Chapter 22

LETTERS FROM PARIS

October 1857

THE SUMMER HAS GONE BUT THE WEATHER IS STILL WONDERFULLY warm.

Uncle Pescott is always angry. Since the dolls' house fête, he shouts at Mamma every day and the servants keep out of his way.

The dolls' house itself has been placed in the library on its stand, and once a week I must dust all the articles in it and return them to their correct places. Sometimes Uncle Pescott watches me, for minutes on end, and I long to throw down my duster and fly from the room. He rarely speaks more than a few words to me, but I may never close the dolls' house until he has inspected every room in it. I wish it had never been built. I hate it.

The summer was the hottest since 1846. Mamma gave us six weeks' holiday from school-work and even Flora ceased to discipline us and spent hours in the orchard every day with only a small piece of needlework that never reached completion.

The son of the Rector of Rindlebridge rode over several times, on his piebald horse, with receipts from his mother for Mamma, or peaches from the Rectory garden.

He was received by Uncle Pescott in the library. Uncle Pes-

cott called him "that carrotty-haired fellow" and spoke dis-
approvingly of his conversation, his clothes and his prospects.

Prue always reported his arrival and Flora was usually walking with Isabella in the drive when he left.

George remarked gravely that it was fortunate that the
library was at the back of the house.

The long, hot days seemed curiously empty. I had grown so
used to Lot that I was always waiting for him to wave from
among the trees, or come stepping down my beech-tree stairs.
Sometimes I wonder if I shall ever grow used to his absence.

He writes to Miss Alder several times a month and always
sends a message to me.

In one letter he talked of a painter called Corot, who has only
recently been noticed by the critics. "His friends call him 'Le
Père Corot'," wrote Lot, "and he lives in a village in the forest
of Fontainebleau. He paints trees and water in the silver light
of the early morning or the evening and I've been told that he
retreats indoors to escape from the bright sunlight of mid-day.
Strange that a painter should not like the sun! Yet Monsieur
Corot is a master, and if I did not love France for her own sake,
I should love her for his."

In another letter Lot wrote: "Delacroix's colours sing like a
choir of angels. It's good to look at other men's work but one
must not look for too long or one would jump in the river. My
own painting, as usual, fills me with despair, but I've completed three small studies of the Seine that are not entirely
horrible."

"So unlike poor Jacopo," said Miss Alder. "He believed each
time that he was painting a masterpiece."

Lot continued in the same letter. "I've learnt a little French,
but still find it simplest when I go shopping to point to what I
want or draw a picture of it and then hand over my purse. The
market women shake with laughter and spread out the coins
they've taken so that I may assure myself that I've not been
cheated.

"Why is the sun in Paris so different from the sun in London? The French sun is gayer, less dusty, more at home. The Emperor of the French loves parks and is himself a landscape gardener. The Bois de Boulogne was a wild forest at the gates of Paris and he's transformed it into a great park. It's one of the glories of Paris—and reminds me of England."

I have heard Lot's letters read aloud so often that I almost know them by heart. Whenever a fresh letter arrives, Miss Alder fetches me to tea in her cottage so that I may receive Lot's message and hear the latest news of him. Lot's letters are the most interesting events of my life and Paris has become, to me, not only a tiny spot on the school-room globe but a great city, with wide and noble streets. How I wish I could see it!

I have been struggling to reform my character—to be less impulsive and less childish and to think, always, before I speak.

I have also been writing a long poem.

These two occupations, together with the school-work for Mamma, now fill my days, so I have little time for my journal.

We no longer have to clean the empty bedrooms at night. Prue and Tom shake out the dust sheets and polish the furniture once a month.

Miss Alder says this is the warmest Autumn for sixteen years.

"That old wheel knew what it were about," says Prue.

Chapter 23

ESCAPE FROM
THE DOLLS' HOUSE

I AM IN DREADFUL DISGRACE.

Uncle Pescott is so furious that he has forbidden Mamma and the others to speak to me.

I am now locked in our bedroom.

I have had no dinner, but George and Harry paid a secret visit to cook and have been pushing biscuits under the door and Isabella has just whispered, through the keyhole, that I may eat her apple in the stocking drawer.

Uncle Pescott ordered Mamma to whip me, but she refused. She has not even reproached me.

It is fortunate that I keep my poems and my journal under the mattress. I have put on my coat and shall write until darkness comes.

Today is Thursday, the dolls' house day, and I knocked on the library door punctually at ten o'clock this morning. I had a clean duster and the little feather broom I always use. "Good morning," I said, and was astonished to observe that Uncle Pescott was smiling. I believe he has not smiled since the day of the fête.

He said, "I have had a very pleasant communication, Lucinda, very pleasant indeed. It is from the Honourable Mrs. Billing. She has just returned from London and intends to give a Hallowe'en party. 'A simple affair,' she says, but one which she hopes will give pleasure to the neighbourhood. She has sent me an invitation which also includes your mother and all of you. She tells me that Lord and Lady Elliston gave just such a party in London last year and the country games with nuts and apples were considered extremely diverting and original. As you all have your new dresses, I shall accept and you may tell your mother and sister the delightful news as soon as you have dusted the dolls' house."

"Yes, Uncle Pescott," I said. I knew it would only enrage him if I said I had no wish to go to Mrs. Billing's party.

"I have sent for your Mamma," said Uncle Pescott, "since she, too, must be informed of the invitation. She must add a brief note to my acceptance. In matters like this, one must study to observe the perfect politeness that Mrs. Billing herself exhibits."

"Yes, Uncle Pescott," I said.

I opened the front of the dolls' house and began to take out, one by one, all the saucepans and kettles from the large kitchen. Since no one ever played with the dolls' house and it remained closed all the week, the tiny utensils were still bright and there was almost no dust for me to remove.

Uncle Pescott came and stood behind me. "The Honourable Mrs. Billing asks if we have any news of that painter fellow," he said.

"He's in France," I said.

"He was a young fool," said Uncle Pescott. "Mrs. Billing is extremely wealthy. He threw away a small fortune."

"Lot didn't wish for a fortune," I said. "He only wished to paint his own pictures."

"He remains a fool," said Uncle Pescott. "A man without money is like a snail without a shell and is at the mercy of every Tom, Dick and Harry who may choose to trample over him. A man *with* money is armed against the world and is never disregarded. I speak from experience."

"Yes, Uncle Pescott," I said and wished he would go back to his desk. His good humour was harder to bear than his usual silence. I thought, too, that Uncle Pescott could never have seen a thrush smashing a snail's shell on a stone. Such a frail protection would not save the snail if Tom, Dick and Harry chose to trample over it.

There was a knock on the library door and Mamma came in, and Uncle Pescott turned from me to repeat the news of Mrs. Billing's invitation.

"It will give Flora and Isabella great pleasure," said Mamma. She did not say that she herself was pleased.

"Tom will ride over with my note of acceptance this morning," said Uncle Pescott, "and you, too, will send a few words of thanks."

"Certainly," said Mamma. "I'll write it at once." She hesitated.

"But there is another thing I need to speak to you about, Mr. Pescott," she said.

"Indeed!" said Uncle Pescott. "Then pray be brief. I've the farm accounts to check and a considerable amount of other work."

"I'm afraid Harry needs new boots," said Mamma.

"Let the old boots be repaired," said Uncle Pescott and began to turn over his papers.

"The old boots are no longer worth repairing," said Mamma. "George wore them until he outgrew them and I saved them for Harry. But now——"

"I provided you all with new costumes in the summer," said Uncle Pescott. "I'm not made of money."

"Must Harry go barefoot then?" said Mamma. "You know, Mr. Pescott, that I can save very little on what you allow me. And the winter is coming," she said with a kind of desperation and I guessed that she was near to tears.

"I suggest that, for once, you yourself provide boots for your son," said Uncle Pescott. "I observe that you are still wearing your locket and gold chain."

I felt my heart leap with anger.

Papa had given Mamma the locket and chain and, apart from her wedding ring, they were all she had left of the small trinkets that had once been hers. The locket was empty, because there had never been money enough to spare for the portrait of Papa that should have been enclosed in it, but engraved on the gold was a bird in a nest defending her young from a snake. Mamma greatly loved the locket and wore it every day.

"I had hoped to keep my locket," she said slowly, "but boots for Harry are more important. No doubt Miss Alder will be able to dispose of it. She has always been a most kind friend. I beg your pardon for troubling you, Mr. Pescott."

And she went away without another word. Uncle Pescott took a step towards the door as though he would have called her back, and I heard him mutter, "Never any end to these demands."

Then he returned to his desk. I believe he had quite forgotten I was in the library. I discovered I was trembling with rage and knelt down quickly in front of the dolls' house. The dolls all seemed to be watching me, with their black, pin-point eyes. They sat stiffly in the drawing-room where we were never allowed to sit and I picked up the Mamma doll. Her locket and chain were represented by a tiny gold lead bead on a single gold embroidery thread and I wondered whether Uncle Pescott would think to remove the toy locket from the doll when Mamma herself no longer wore the real locket.

I was sick with grief for Mamma and contempt for Uncle Pescott.

I put the Mamma doll back on the sofa in the dolls' house drawing-room, where Uncle Pescott had ordered it to sit, and picked up the doll that represented me. The small wooden creature had shiny red cheeks and an expression of silly astonishment, and I only knew she was mine by the turquoise sash and simple dress. She was so tiny I could hold her between my finger and thumb. Uncle Pescott must have heard me move, because he said sharply, "I shall be grateful if you will finish your dusting and leave the library."

"I was thinking," I said.

"There is no need for you to think here," said Uncle Pescott. "Finish your work and go."

"I don't stop thinking when I come into the library," I said, "and I was thinking that you'd have to remove the Mamma doll's locket. Had you thought of that, Uncle Pescott?"

"Finish your work and leave the room," said Uncle Pescott.

"I've scarcely begun my work," I said. "I was wondering, too, Uncle Pescott, whether my doll likes living in your dolls' house."

Uncle Pescott stood up and took a step towards me.

"I believe my doll hates it," I said, "as much as I hate living in your house, Uncle Pescott. We might all have been happy, but you trample over us as you please."

For a moment Uncle Pescott appeared to be speechless with rage and I quickly shut the dolls' house and walked, with my doll, over to the fire.

"You told Mrs. Billing that we each possessed our own doll," I said, "so I can do what I choose with mine. And I'm going to set her free, Uncle Pescott, and you can't stop me."

"Have you taken leave of your senses?" cried Uncle Pescott. "Give the doll to me, Lucinda!"

"No," I said. "If I caught a bird in one of these great rooms, I should run out into the garden and open my hands. And the bird would fly away. But this poor doll is only wood and can't fly, and if I hide her, you'll make me put her back in the dolls' house. There are too many prisoners in the Manor, Uncle Pescott, so I'm going to let my doll escape."

Uncle Pescott was coming towards me.

"Are you quite mad?" he shouted. "Put the doll back at once. Do you hear me? I order you to put the doll back."

"No," I said. "I can't escape myself but my doll can."

And I dropped her in the smoke at the back of the flaming logs.

The fire wrapped her round and in an instant she was gone.

Chapter 24

SMOKE ON HALLOWE'EN

MISS ALDER HAS SOLD MAMMA'S LOCKET AND CHAIN AND HARRY
has his new boots and there is even money left for future needs.
Yet I could weep for Mamma's loss.

She had a habit of feeling for her locket as she talked and her
hand still flies up to the place where it used to be. Dear Miss
Alder has so arranged it that both the locket and chain may be
redeemed at any time. I dream of selling my poem—I have nothing else I can sell—but have no idea how such a thing is done.

I am not to be allowed to go to Mrs. Billing's Hallowe'en
party. And I may never enter the library again. Uncle Pescott
cannot guess that I am thankful for both these punishments.
But Isabella is less pleased. It is she who will now have to dust
the dolls' house.

October 31st

It is All Hallow's Eve and I am alone in the Manor, locked
into the school-room with my journal and my supper on a tray.
I had not expected to have to remain entirely by myself, but this
is a further punishment, for burning my doll. The servants who
sleep here have all been sent to the village.

I believe I am not afraid, although it is a strange, sultry night for October and the smoke from the fire sometimes makes me cough. It is a wretched fire, half choked with slack. But I have a candle and can write quietly until Mamma comes back.

Mamma herself would not have prepared for the party if she had known what Uncle Pescott intended. He said nothing beforehand, but turned the key in the lock and informed Mamma, when she would have come into the school-room to say "Goodbye" to me, that the key was in his pocket and that he did not intend to unlock the door until he returned.

"I've sent the servants off," he said, "but instructed them to be back by ten o'clock. Lucinda will remain where she is until I let her out. That will, perhaps, teach her——"

He and Mamma were in the corridor just outside the school-room door but I did not hear the end of the sentence because Mamma interrupted him, saying quickly that she would not allow me to stay alone in an empty house but would, herself, remain with me.

"The carriages are waiting," said Uncle Pescott sharply, "and we should be on our way."

He must have walked off down the stairs, because Mamma called to me that she was going after him to try to get the key and that she would be back almost immediately.

I ran to one of the windows but could see little of what was happening in the drive below. But I heard Uncle Pescott's impatient voice.

"Very well, we will discuss it in the carriage. We can't stand arguing in the drive. Get in!"

I believe he must have played a cruel trick on Mamma and given a signal for the carriages to start, I heard a carriage door slam and at once they drove off.

I know Mamma will not leave me alone for long, but I cannot imagine how she will persuade Uncle Pescott to allow her to return. Already she has been gone for more than half an hour. I have been poking the fire but it only smokes the more.

Prue says that on Hallowe'en if you eat an apple before a

looking-glass you will see your true love peeping over your shoulder in the mirror. She swore she saw Tom last year and hopes to see him again tonight.

I heard Tom laughing with her this morning. (How long ago it seems!) Tom said that if she would tell him at what time in the evening she intended to eat her apple he would certainly be there and hoped she would give him half of it.

"Ah, but that's what that Eve in the Bible did," said Prue, "and there weren't no good come of it."

The smoke hurts my eyes. I hope Mamma will not be too long.

Prue says that this is the night when all kinds of spirits walk abroad and one may even call them to come. I should never dare to do that for fear one did come. I wonder if poor Mrs. Marden has ever called her Sophie. I suppose not—since she still believes that Sophie is alive and will come back. I should not like to be up in the woods alone on a black night like this. There is not a star to be seen and there is a strange heaviness in the air. Twice I have had to open the window to let the smoke escape.

Now I shall eat my supper.

An hour has gone and still Mamma has not come.

The smoke drifts down the chimney and spreads through the room so that at times I can scarcely breathe. I keep opening the windows, but the last time I did it, the candle went out and I could not, at first, find the matches to re-light it. I knew there was nothing to be afraid of in the dark and yet I was afraid.

Why is Mamma so long?

If I occupy my mind, the time will pass more quickly. I must keep on writing.

I wish Lot were here. Do ghosts walk in Paris on Hallowe'en or is it only here, in the country places, that people believe such stories?

The picture Lot gave me is still in the drawer under my petticoats. If I had known Uncle Pescott would lock me up, I believe I should have brought it in here when I fetched my journal after tea. I wish I could look at it and remember that sweet spring morning. I wish Lot were here. I had grown so used to him and was so comfortable with him that I still seem always to be waiting for him to appear. He was my friend, but he went away. I shall repeat to myself all that I can recollect of his letters. I shall keep on repeating them, until Mamma comes back.

Nearly an hour and a half has gone. It is difficult to write because I am listening, all the time, for the sound of carriage wheels. Why is Mamma so long? She promised she would come back. The smoke is dreadful but I must keep on writing.

I have opened both the windows at the top. The darkness outside seems to press against the glass and would come into the school-room if it could. My candle is burning with a long flame. I must trim it.

Why doesn't Mamma come? How long must I wait?

There is barely an inch of candle left.

I have been sitting under the table thinking of my little doll. I dropped her among the flames and smoke at the back of the library fire and now I myself am—But I will not think such thoughts. I must listen for the carriage wheels. If only I could hear the key turn in the lock and Mamma's voice outside the door! If only——

Keep on writing. But how can I write and listen? Mamma, come quickly!

Some time ago I tried to break open the door. The candle will go out in a few minutes. I cannot bear to be alone in the darkness and smoke, so I must escape—I must get out of this room.

There are two wooden bars across each window, but perhaps I can burn——

Chapter 25

FIRE ON HALLOWE'EN: LION COTTAGE

November 1857

THIS EVENING I AM LESS UNHAPPY.

I have fetched my journal and I intend to write down all the things that occurred on Hallowe'en as plainly and exactly as I can recollect them.

Yet even now, as I take up my pencil, I begin to tremble.

Miss Alder and I are sitting by her parlour fire and the lamp gives a clear steady light and, from time to time, Miss Alder says, "Listen to this, Lucinda", and reads me a few lines from her favourite, Mr. Thackeray.

And nothing I can wish or say or do, will change, in the smallest degree, the events of All Hallow's night.

If only one could step back in time for a few days, for a week perhaps, and undo the past! Or shut one's eyes and force events to change! Or wake in the morning and discover that one had only been lost in some dreadful dream! But I was so much afraid there seemed nothing else I could do.

I *had* to escape from the school-room before the candle went out. Miss Alder says I was not to blame, but Uncle Pescott will never forgive me, or see me again.

There were two wooden bars across each of the school-room windows. Mr. Pryor had fixed them there when we first came to the Manor, because we were still young and Mamma was afraid one of us might lean out too far and fall.

I cannot tell how long I was alone, in the locked school-room, on Hallowe'en. It was so long that the night became strange and full of terror and although I struggled to act calmly and do only what was necessary, I believe I behaved without proper consideration for Uncle Pescott's property.

I thought of only one thing—that I should die, in the darkness and smoke, if I did not escape.

It appeared to me that if I could burn through the top bar of the left-hand window, I could climb on to the sill and jump down on the flat space behind the two great stone urns over the porch.

My desperation made this plan seem possible. The cupboard where we kept our school books, and a few old toys, had layers of paper on the shelves, and I threw the books on to the floor, rolled several sheets of paper into a torch and lit it at the flickering candle-flame. Then I held the torch under one end of the wooden bar.

The torch burned quickly, flaring against the glass, and flakes of blackened paper fell to the ground.

I recollected afterwards that I heard the glass crack.

I made a number of torches, one after the other. There was a smell of burning varnish and then, suddenly, the bar was alight, with small flames curling round it and running along its whole length. I quickly flung up the window.

The candle seemed about to go out but now I had this other light. I fumbled at the bottom of the cupboard and found our three old skipping ropes and knotted them together and tied the end of the line round my waist. Then I pushed the table to the window and fastened the other end to one of the table legs.

I thought, in a kind of dream, that if I slipped from the sill I

150

should hang against the Manor wall, like a spider on its thread, until Mamma came home.

I think then the candle went out.

The night air that came in through the open window refreshed me a little although there was no breath of wind, and I felt for my journal and flung it out into the drive. Then I climbed on the table and kicked furiously at the burning wooden bar. Several small flames danced up the edge of the righthand curtain but I paid no attention to them. I kept on kicking the bar until it broke up in a blaze of sparks.

I cannot clearly remember what happened after that, but I must have crept from the table over the lower bar and on to the sill, because I found myself sitting on the sill holding tightly to the lefthand curtain. Still clutching the curtain, I wriggled to the edge of the sill. Then I let go and leapt sideways down on to the flat roof of the porch and fell on my hands and knees behind one of the great stone urns.

It would have been an easy jump in daylight, but with only the fiery curtain to light me, I was so terrified that I scarcely dared move again and stayed panting on my knees until suddenly I realised that I was no longer a prisoner.

Then I got to my feet, broke the glass of the corridor window with my shoe, unfastened the window and climbed back into the house. I felt for the matches on the corridor table and lighted the candle there.

The familiar closed doors, the sound of the clock quietly ticking on the wall and the pattern of roses on the corridor carpet brought me back to myself for a few seconds, and I was distressed and horrified by the broken glass on the floor.

But I had not escaped from the fearful strangeness of the night by escaping from the school-room. As I began to untie the skipping ropes from my waist, I discovered that the rope that had been fastened to the table leg was loose and burned through. A curious flickering light was showing under the school-room door.

I knew then that the house was on fire.

I thought, "I must run for help," and then, "But where can I run?" Rindle Green had no fire engine and Ramsford, which had one, was seven miles away. And already small flames were thrusting under the school-room door, towards the edge of the corridor carpet. I rushed to our bedroom, set the candle on the floor in the doorway, carried out two water jugs and flung all the water at the school-room door and over the carpet. Then I hurried to Mamma's room and the boys' room, and emptied their jugs along the length of the corridor.

I could think of nothing else to do.

There was still one jug left in our room and I poured the water over the top of the staircase. Then I remembered my picture and hurried back to our bedroom, set the candle on one of the wash-hand-stands and opened the petticoat drawer. As I felt under the petticoats, I thought, "I can save these too. And I must save my poems and my new dress."

I opened the bedroom window and threw an armful of petticoats down into the garden. I set my picture and my poems aside, to be carried to safety and after that, opened all the other drawers (Flora's and Isabella's as well as mine) and the two great wardrobes and tossed our old dresses and underclothes, our stockings and shoes, our jackets and summer bonnets, all out of the window. Luckily the painted fan was safe, because Isabella had taken it with her to the party.

When I had finished in our room, I hurried to Mamma's and emptied her drawers and wardrobe in the same way. I discovered, however, one small drawer that contained a packet of Papa's letters tied with white ribbon, and several of his compositions for the pianoforte, and these, with other small family mementoes and Mamma's few books, I wrapped in an old shawl to he carried downstairs with my picture.

A smell of scorched and burning wood seemed to fill the house. The school-room door was alight.

I fled to the boys' room and began to fling their clothes out of the window. When I discovered Papa's watch, I wrapped it, with the other precious things, in the old shawl.

(I know now that by opening the windows I helped spread the fire.)

I cannot tell how long I spent throwing our property out into the garden. I believe I worked quickly, with a kind of desperate resolution to save all I could. But I watched to see that there was time for me to escape down the staircase.

The five empty bedrooms were locked and so were Uncle Pescott's bedroom and dressingroom. And I dared not climb to the servants' quarters for fear the fire should trap me under the roof.

I tried to save the clock on the corridor wall, but the heat from the blazing school-room door drove me back.

I can scarcely write this without shuddering. When it seemed that I had done all I could, I twisted the old shawl into a bundle and struggled with it down the stairs. The flames of the burning door lit the top of the stairs, but in the entrance hall it was so dark I had to find and light the candle on the hall table before I could unbolt the front door. As I carried my bundle out on to the step, it suddenly struck me that I had saved only our property, and was leaving Uncle Pescott's to burn.

I had a fearful dread that the fire might suddenly sweep down the stairs and engulf me, but I picked up the candle and stumbled into the drawing-room. The picture of the little children with the toy cart was too big for me to move, but I collected all the ornaments and the clock on the mantlepiece and went back a second time for a small chair and a lamp. After that I dared stay no longer. Already the fire had reached the top of the stairs.

I carried everything down the steps into the drive and slammed the front door behind me.

I can write no more tonight.

Miss Alder says it is my bedtime. The kettle is steaming on the hob and I shall have hot water to add to the cold water in my bedroom jug.

I have a small fire too in my bedroom.

Miss Alder has hung my picture on the bedroom wall so that it is the first thing I see when I wake in the morning and the last thing I see at night. I believe I have never been so comfortable and never so distressed. I wish Lot were here. Perhaps he would make me laugh again.

Chapter 26

THE STORM

I HAD NO DIFFICULTY IN FINDING MY JOURNAL IN THE DRIVE. THE glare from the school-room windows lit every pebble with fiery light and even the smoke that hung over the roof was touched with dreadful red.

I set aside my picture and poems, and carried my bundle and Uncle Pescott's lamp to the summer-house. Then I began to gather up the piles of clothes under our bedroom windows.

Already the flames, like living creatures, were peering out of our room and had reached one of the attics. The smoke had increased. It rolled from the open windows and was sometimes all round me so that I had to turn away and cover my eyes. I found my coat and bonnet and put them with my picture and journal. I lost count of the number of journeys I made to the summer-house. I heaped as many clothes as I could on the rustic chairs and laid the rest on the floor. Mamma's mementoes and her books and Papa's watch I placed on the rustic table. The watch, which George always wound, showed twenty minutes past nine.

Lastly, I packed into the summer-house the clock, the chair, and the ornaments I had saved for Uncle Pescott. By that time, I think about a third of the roof was alight.

I put on my coat and bonnet and tore a page from my journal. I had forgotten to save my pencil from the school-room, but found a stump in my pocket. I always collect small pieces of pencil. I wrote a note by the light of the flames.

My Dear, Dear Mamma,

The fire was my fault and I couldn't put it out. Uncle Pescott will know that only I'm to blame. I'm quite safe.

Your loving daughter,

LUCINDA.

I tucked the note under Papa's watch.

I had meant to walk to the village and ask Miss Alder what I should do, but I felt suddenly so weak with exhaustion that I believed I could never reach Miss Alder's cottage. I thought, "I must find a place to sleep," and turned and began to walk up the garden. I climbed High Meadow very slowly, because I was so tired. When, at last, I sat down in my armchair among the beech roots, I believed I should stay there till morning. I tucked my hands in the sleeves of my coat, leaned back and fell asleep at once. I have no idea how long I slept.

I had not expected the storm. I woke to a fierce lightning flash over High Meadow and a crack of thunder that was like great rocks tumbling from a mountain. I got to my feet quickly, tucked my journal and poems under my arm and picked up my picture. I have always hated thunder.

The rain came almost at once, first a few drops and then a torrent. It beat down from the black sky and the noise of it was like some great cascading river that had overflowed the heavens. And when the lightning flashed, it seemed that the air itself had been turned to white, pouring water.

I could not stay in my armchair. My feet knew the way up my root stairs and I stumbled through the bushes and into the wood. Mamma had always told us that we should never shelter under trees during a thunderstorm, but I was too desperate to care about the danger. I knew this part of the woods so well that I thought I could easily find a hollow where I could cover myself with drifted leaves and hide from the storm. But I had never before been out in the woods at night.

The lightning transformed them so strangely that I lost all sense of direction and stumbled about as though I were straying in some wild, unknown forest. The forked lightning ran down behind the branches and the sheet lightning lit the great trunks with violet light and spread bewildering, inky shadows down the slopes. And when the darkness returned, after each flash, I fell over the roots and walked into the trees.

And all the time, the thunder rolled and cracked overhead and the rain beat down through the roof of the wood.

And I went on and on.

In the end, I was so distracted by weariness and terror that I forgot why I was there, or what I was looking for. But when I came suddenly to Mrs. Marden's hut, and the glare of the lightning showed me where I was, I fell on my knees and crawled in at the low doorway. I could see nothing, but the hut was warm and fairly dry. I smelt bracken and dead leaves, and putting out my hand, touched Mrs. Marden's shoulder. She murmured something, in a sleepy voice, but did not wake. (I marvel now that she could have slept through the storm, but I suppose she had grown used to all kinds of weather.) I said, "May I stay here, Mrs. Marden? I'm afraid of the thunder," and heard her roll over.

"Eh, Sophie," she said. "But you're a great girl now. And it's not yet morning."

"But it's thundering," I said.

"Ah, yes. You were always feared of the thunder," said Mrs. Marden, and as the lightning flashed again, I saw how she pushed back the bracken as though she were pushing back a blanket.

"Eh, well! Come in then, child," she said. "Come in." Then her voice changed and I was glad of the darkness. "I was dreaming you were a little child again," she said. "You've been a long time gone, Sophie."

I took off my bonnet and managed to unbutton my wet coat and push it aside. Then I wriggled down beside her under the bracken. I remember nothing more of that night. . . .

When I woke, the morning had come, but it was still half dark and Mrs. Marden was asleep. I lay a few moments recollecting where I was. It was a dreadful waking. But I knew that I must slip away at once, before Mrs. Marden woke, because she had believed me to be her Sophie and it would be cruel to let her discover the truth. I felt for my picture and my poems and journal and my wet coat and bonnet. Then I softly drew away from her and crawled out of the hut.

In the grey light of dawn the oaks stood like stiff giants, black and still strange, not the friendly trees of daylight that I knew. And everywhere was silence, except for the sound of dripping and the rustle of my own footsteps. I dragged on my coat but

it was so sodden it made me shiver and I took it off again. I hung my soaked bonnet on my arm. The rain had stopped and it was a mild morning, but the woods seemed half-drowned and everywhere was the sorrowful smell of autumn.

I believed I was separated from all my previous life. The events of the night before seemed like a high wall that cut me off from Mamma and all the others. There was great comfort in belonging to a family, but now I was outside that comfort because I had done a fearful thing. I was truly alone and even Mamma would never be able to draw me back into my old place.

I understood then how poor vagabonds and thieves must feel, cut off from the world of law-abiding, gentle people. It is terrible to be an outcast. I felt my heart was almost breaking.

Then I remembered Miss Alder. I had meant to go to her the night before and would go that morning. "She'll tell me what to do," I thought, "and she'll carry a message to Mamma." It appeared to me that I must not, myself, go near Mamma for fear Uncle Pescott might blame her and send her and the others away.

I hurried on through the wood as the light grew clearer, and when I came to the familiar hazel bushes, I pushed through them and climbed down to my chair.

I thought it was still too early to walk to the village and knock on Miss Alder's door, and I had nowhere else to go. I rolled up my coat into a cushion and sat down on it. It was very damp, but not as damp as the armchair. The huge roots round me were still dark and streaked with wet. I kept my eyes lowered because I dared not look at the valley or the Manor. I had begun to shiver and my left arm hurt, and I discovered that my sleeve was torn and there was a long gash above my elbow. I noticed it and forgot it. My shivering had grown so violent that I scarcely knew what to do. I pressed my knees together, clasped my arms round them and shut my eyes. I remained like that for some time.

I did not know that Mrs. Marden had come down my steps until she stood beside me. She said, "I've seen you here before, Miss, haven't I? You're Miss Lucinda, aren't you? I must tell you my good news."

I looked up at her. In the morning light, she appeared worn and very ill, but she was smiling with a kind of prim joy and the wildness had gone from her face.

"My Sophie came back last night," she said. "My Sophie came back."

"I'm very glad, Mrs. Marden," I said.

"She was gone again this morning, but I didn't expect her to stay," said Mrs. Marden. "She was always set on seeing the world. She came into my bed and when I woke her place was still warm. She was always feared of thunder and she went away, you see, Miss, when the storm was over. But she's a good girl and knows I'll not worry any more. I'm off to the village now. This is for you, Miss. I was saving it for my Sophie, but she doesn't need it and it's of no use to me." She put an old tea-caddy down beside me. "You favour my Sophie, Miss. I've always thought so. My mind's at rest now I've seen my girl, and I must go and clean my windows and doorstep. That Miss Alder will be glad to hear my news. Good morning, Miss."

And she turned quickly and strode away up my steps before I could thank her.

The day was brightening.

I sat staring at the tea-caddy, thinking of only one thing—that I must look at the Manor. "Look now," I told myself. "Look now!"

But I still sat with my head averted.

"I must know what I've done," I thought. "I must know."

I forced myself to stand up and quickly opened my eyes.

The Manor still stood—yet it was changed. One side was almost roofless, with empty holes where the windows had been. The heavy beams of the attics still reared up over black-ened walls and a thin haze of smoke hung over them, scarcely moving under the pale morning sky. It was a fearful sight. The rain must have put out the flames before the whole Manor was destroyed, but even the undamaged part was so darkened by smoke and rain that the house seemed a strange and desolate ruin, set in the sweet valley I knew so well. I could not bear to look at it and hid my eyes.

"No one will ever forgive me," I thought. "I shall have to creep away and hide in some secret place." And such an anguish of despair took hold of me that I feared I should faint and had quickly to sit down again.

When I dared to look again, there were men on the roof and groups of people everywhere round the Manor, staring, pointing, running here and there and shouting.

Chapter 27

ALL SAINTS' DAY

I CROUCHED DOWN IN MY ARMCHAIR WHEN I SAW ALL THE PEOPLE round the Manor. I was afraid I might be observed. The early morning light filled the valley and I recollected that it was the first day of November and All Saints' Day. The sun was a small, white disc that brightened every second.

"But I must be a child of darkness," I thought and the sense of desolation was almost more than I could bear. "If only Lot were here," I said to myself. "I should not feel so entirely alone. Lot would have been unaware of the great wall between me and other people," and I imagined him saying in his anxious half-exasperated voice, "But you're not going to cry *again*, are you, Lucinda?" Even as I recollected this, the tears began to run down my cheeks and I covered my face with my hands.

I tried to conjure up Lot and his sketch-book but my tears continued to drip through my fingers into my lap and I feared they might flow for ever.

I wept and wept. And then suddenly, a shawl was wrapped round my shoulders and Prue was stooping over me.

"So this is where you got to, Miss Luce," she said.

"Oh, Prue," I said. "Oh, Prue——"

"Me and Tom thought all on a sudden, that you was here," said Prue in her usual cheerful voice. "But me and Tom didn't say a word to anyone for fear we was wrong. Why, you look like a scarecrow, Miss Luce, as have been blown on and rained on and pushed on a bonfire. Now, you must come to your Mamma."

"How did you know—" I began.

"Me and Tom is doin' a bit of courtin'," said Prue, "and now and then we takes a walk in the woods. We seen you several times, Miss Luce, but Tom said it weren't no business of ours. Now I must just give a bit of a shout, so Tom can run to the Lodge and tell your Mamma you're safe. Tom's watchin' down by the orchard wall."

"But, Prue," I said, "I don't want Uncle Pescott to think that Mamma——"

"He'll think this and he'll think that and nothin' won't stop the Squire thinkin' what he wants to think," said Prue. "And there's your poor Mamma been druv nearly frantic with worry. Now, don't you dare say another word, Miss Luce."

She stepped back on to the root stairs and gave such a great shout that it seemed to echo all across the valley. And an answering shout came back from the orchard.

"Now your poor Mamma will be able to swallow a bit o' breakfast," said Prue. "And don't forget your picture and the old tea-caddy. Here, I'll carry them. This caddy's a pretty fair weight. What's in it, Miss Luce?"

"I don't know," I said. "Mrs. Marden gave it to me."

I could scarcely walk, and Prue had to help me up into the wood. I went with her, because I knew, suddenly, that I could not go away from Mamma and the others.

That was ten days ago.

As we came down High Meadow, people began to run towards us. Prue was supporting me and I scarcely noticed them at first. I had been counting my steps, in an effort to overcome my trembling, but the shouting and cheering made me pause for a moment and look up.

George came charging up the slope and behind him came Flora and Isabella, with Harry panting behind. And after them

164

came a crowd of villagers, with Mr. Pryor at their head. George almost flung himself at me.

"Oh, Luce, you gave us a dreadful fright," he shouted. "The men have been looking for you all night. We thought you'd run away."

"Mamma was quite distracted. You deserve to be whipped," cried Flora, and Isabella added, "Mrs. Billing would have kept Mamma for the night, because she was prostrate with her headache, but she insisted on returning at once with us. And when she discovered your note, she walked back to the village, calling to you all the way, because she believed you must have set out for London."

"Miss Alder drove her back to the Lodge and is still with her," said Flora.

"There's blood on your sleeve," wailed Harry. "Are you going to die?"

"No," I said.

"You know you should be called 'Cinda', not Luce," said George in the serious voice he always uses when he makes a joke. "Now we'll take you to Mamma."

I stood with my head hanging, ashamed and quite exhausted, and yet with a kind of comfort creeping into my mind. The great wall that I had thought would separate me from them for ever was not there. They were all round me and I was still one of them. Flora was as cross and Harry as tender-hearted as usual and George could still make a joke about my name.

"Tom shouted that you were safe before he ran to the Lodge to tell Mamma, but she won't be happy until she sees you," said Flora sharply. "Now do come along, Luce. We ought to wash you first, but I suppose Mamma will still recognise you although most people would take you for a beggar girl. What have you done to your arm?"

"I must have cut it on the broken glass," I said. "I had to break the corridor window. I had to get out of the school-room window because I was afraid I should die in the smoke."

"So you burnt down half the Manor to make sure that you didn't," said Flora. "Really, Luce, you are *ridiculously* stupid. Why didn't you pick up the fire in the shovel and throw it out of the window?"

"I didn't think of it," I said.

"You *never* think," said Flora. "Now *do* come along. Can you walk as far as the Lodge?"

"Yes," I said.

Prue's hand was under my right elbow and George held my hurt arm carefully and firmly. "I expect Mamma will be coming. I'll run and meet her," said Harry.

There were villagers all about us and I heard them murmuring together as we began slowly to make our way down towards the orchard gate.

"They *do* say the Squire locked her in."

"They *do* say he rushed about like a mad thing, when he came home and find the Manor half gone."

"It's a judgement on him—that's what *I* say."

"The carriages was caught by the storm comin' back. They *do* say the bridge at Rindlebridge were under water and they had to go round by Reyne. The young ladies and their Mamma was quite desperate."

"Here's the Squire comin'."

I saw Uncle Pescott rushing up the slope and his enraged face seemed almost as dark as his clothes.

He was carrying his ebony stick and he swung it up, as he came near, as though he would strike me into the earth.

And then, suddenly, I was surrounded, walled about by people. George and Prue were in front of me, and Flora and Isabella on each side, and round us all were the villagers crowded together, jostling quietly and saying nothing but making a strong barrier between Uncle Pescott and me.

I heard Mr. Pryor say, "O no, sir. *That* won't do," and Prue cry out, "For shame, sir! Miss Luce haven't had no breakfast and is as weak and tremblin' as a bit o' totty grass."

"Let me through," shouted Uncle Pescott. "Let me through. I wish to speak to my niece."

But no one moved and I felt so ill I had to sit down on the ground.

Flora stooped and said, "Don't you dare be sick, Luce," and I shook my head and shut my eyes. And for a moment it seemed curious that it was Uncle Pescott who was outside the wall and not I. But the thought slipped out of my mind at once and Uncle Pescott's shouting seemed to come from a great distance away.

I think it was Miss Alder's voice that brought me to myself. I heard her say, "Good morning, Mr. Pescott. I've just come from the Lodge and your sister-in-law is on her way here. Now I believe I must beg for the loan of your stick. My rheumatism is a little troublesome this morning. Ah, thank you! Now where *is* Lucinda?"

There was a whispering and shuffling all round us, and then dear Miss Alder was bending over me. "We have all been greatly concerned about you, my dear," she said. "Now, can you stand up?" Uncle Pescott's stick was tucked under her arm.

I cannot clearly recall what happened after that. I believe we passed through a lane of people and they seemed all to be smiling. Only Uncle Pescott did not smile. He was standing alone and he stepped forward and barred our way. I shall never forget his words.

"You are a wicked, wicked girl, Lucinda," he said. "You are uncontrolled, vindictive and destructive and I will no longer support you or be responsible for you. I intend to put you in the charge of the housekeeper in my London house. You will work as a maid there, sleep with the other maids and earn your keep. You will leave for London this afternoon and I shall take you there myself. After that I hope never to set eyes on you again."

I believe I shrank away from him.

"My dear sir," said Miss Alder, "arrangements for Lucinda's immediate future are already made. I've discussed the matter with her mother. Lucinda will come to me. No—pray, don't say a word, Mr. Pescott."

There was a strange silence, for a moment. Then Miss Alder continued, "I understand there is room for your sister-in-law and four children at the Lodge. You yourself will doubtless wish to remain at the Manor while it is being re-built. I'm told that both the library and your upstairs rooms are undamaged. How fortunate it is that you have the dolls' house to refer to!

"As for Lucinda—she will, of course, join her sisters and brothers at the Lodge every afternoon for the lessons with her mother. I will myself fetch her every evening. I shall be glad of her company at Lion Cottage. As one grows older one discovers the world afresh through those who are still young."

I listened in a kind of dream. "Such a beautiful morning," said Miss Alder. "Ah, I was almost forgetting. I must return your stick, Mr. Pescott. Thank you, but I believe I can manage quite well without it after all. Come, Lucinda."

High Meadow shone in the pale November sunlight and the villagers followed us down towards the orchard. "I should not have kept you standing so long," said Miss Alder, "but there are times when one must speak firmly."

"Yes," I said, "I understand. It's All Saints' Day, isn't it? All the old, holy saints are dead but I think, perhaps, there are still a number of people who——"

Then the orchard gate opened and Mamma came quickly up the path and I forgot what I was going to say and went to meet her.

Chapter 28

PURCHASES IN THE PARLOUR

POOR MRS. MARDEN DIED ON ALL SAINTS' DAY. SHE SHARED HER bed with me and yet I had to creep away without thanking her. And she gave me all the money she had saved for Sophie, in the old tea-caddy.

As she hurried to the village on All Saints' morning she met half the villagers streaming along the road to the Manor. News of the fire had caused wonderful excitement in Rindle Green and all those who could spare the time wished to see the ruined house for themselves.

As Mrs. Marden passed each group she called out joyfully that her Sophie had come back in the night and that now she was going to tell the good news to Miss Alder. Several people tried to make her understand that Miss Alder was at the Lodge with Mamma, but she refused to listen and hurried on.

When Mrs. Marden reached the village the baker's wife (who had had to stay at home because she has a young baby), saw her knocking at Miss Alder's door, and observing her changed expression and curious excitement, begged her to come into her own kitchen and sit down.

Mrs. Marden replied that she could not sit down because she had to clean her doorstep and windows, as soon as she had spoken to Miss Alder.

The baker's wife knew that Mrs. Marden's cottage was half-derelict and, having no idea what to do, picked up her baby and ran to find the rector.

He was too late. When he reached Miss Alder's cottage he found the door open and Mrs. Marden leaning back in the arm-chair in the kitchen. It seemed that she had, after all, sat down to wait. Her hands were folded under her cloak and her bare feet were on the fender. She was dead but still smiling to herself.

Most of the villagers attended her funeral, because she had always belonged to Rindle Green. But Miss Alder stayed with me.

There were a hundred and twenty-three gold sovereigns in the tea-caddy. I made a package of them and wrote a note to Uncle Pescott begging him to use the money to help pay for the repairs to the Manor. Miss Alder took the note and the money to the Manor. Uncle Pescott read my note, threw it in the library fire and said there was no reply. He sent back the package unopened. So now I am very rich.

Yet it is terrible to be hated as Uncle Pescott hates me. I tried to give the money to Mamma, but she said I should ask Miss Alder to take charge of it for me.

The re-building of the Manor has begun. Uncle Pescott was not deterred by the thought that frost and snow might come later in the winter and workmen have been called in not only from Rindle Green and Rindlebridge but from Reyne and Ramsford. And an architect has been brought down from London to oversee the whole work of restoration.

Prue says his office is in the small parlour where the dolls' house was built.

"You done the Squire a good turn, Miss Luce," said Prue. "He's got his mind occupied again, like it were when he were took up with that dolls' house. And you done us servants a good turn too. We gets a bit o' peace these days although we're run off our feet. It's the workmen and the poor gentleman from London that is fair druv mad. The Squire's here, there and everywhere, prancin' round with his old rolls o' drawin's, always checkin' and inspectin' this and that. Anyone ud think the Manor come out o' his own head, doors and windows and all."

I have been walking to the Lodge every afternoon for my lessons. It is wonderfully comfortable to sit round the table with Mamma and the others and I believe that one day I shall write some paragraphs for a newspaper on the delights of belonging to a family.

When I go to my lessons Miss Alder usually accompanies me as far as the hawthorn tree that is half-way along the road and there Flora and Isabella or George and Harry meet me.

Miss Alder always fetches me back in her gig, after tea. I have grown very fond of her little horse Thimble. We are extremely peaceful at the Lodge in the afternoons. Uncle Pescott never leaves the Manor and although Mamma has a great deal to attend to there in the mornings she has had none of her dreadful headaches lately. Uncle Pescott is so fully occupied with the repairs that he has little time for household matters. And that is a great blessing.

On the first afternoon I returned to school, Flora and Isabella met me and Flora said she had something to explain to me.

"Yes?" I said a little apprehensively.

"I want you to understand, Luce, that we didn't know you'd been left quite alone on Hallowe'en," said Flora. "We thought the servants were there. And we'd no idea you'd been locked in the school-room. If we had known I should have ordered our carriage to turn back. As for our beloved Uncle—when Mamma insisted on returning, he was quite astounded to discover that he'd inadvertently put the school-room key in his pocket."

Suddenly Flora stood still in the middle of the road and clenched her fists. "If only we were free of him!" she cried. "It's monstrous that we and Mamma should be dependent on him. If only he'd go away! Oh, Luce, Luce, I can't endure the sight of him and I dread the time when we shall have to go back to the Manor. If only a thunderbolt would fall on it! If only Uncle Pescott would settle in London!"

"If a thunderbolt fell on the Manor Uncle Pescott would only re-build it," said Isabella.

"Yes," said Flora. "He'd re-build it. Every stone would be put back in its place and every pane of glass. And the two urns would stand precisely where they stood before."

And she began to walk along the road at such a furious pace that Isabella and I had great difficulty in keeping up with her.

"Why are gentlemen so different?" cried Flora. "Why? I didn't understand how different they could be until——"

"Until the gentleman without the two carriages came," I said.

"He hasn't even one," said Flora, desperately. "And, oh Luce, his hair is the colour of carrots and yet I can't help——"

And she flew on ahead while Isabella and I followed panting.

"Poor Flora!" said Isabella.

"Being a young lady in love seems to be very difficult," I said.

I have decided that on December 4th, my birthday, I shall give a surprise present to Mamma and each of the others. I have never spent money before—because I have never had any—and I feel it is a very serious undertaking.

As usual I have consulted Miss Alder. George and Harry will each receive a cricket bat and a ball, and Flora and Isabella, since they seem always to long for new clothes, will each have a new winter hat, which Miss Alder will design and make. We have worn bonnets all our lives and none of us has ever had a hat before.

Mamma's present will be best of all and even to write of it gives me pleasure. I asked Miss Alder if she could buy back Mamma's locket for me and she smiled. "I fear, Lucinda, I must let you into a secret," she said.

Then she went into her work-room and came back with a

locked metal box. She opened it on the parlour table and inside were a number of small packages wrapped in tissue paper, which she lifted out carefully and opened one by one.

And I could scarcely believe my eyes.

There was the locket, with the courageous bird defending her young from the snake, and there were the cameo brooch and filigree bracelet, the silver vinaigrette and small watch and all Mamma's other familiar trinkets that I had looked at and touched and admired when I was very small.

With a curious sensation of joy I recognised them all. They were of no great value but were part of our early memories and of the time when our Papa was alive and we had never heard of Rindle Green.

"I knew your Mamma would never accept direct help," said Miss Alder. "So I purchased these myself and hoped that one day she might be able to redeem them. Here is the list of what I paid for each item. You see, Lucinda, I've always kept exact accounts of all my business transactions. My father used to say I'd a far better head for figures than he. Well now, you'd like to purchase the locket and chain?"

She spoke with a sudden briskness, as though she were about to sell me a packet of pins or a yard of ribbon, and I understood that she was trying to prevent me from thanking her. So I simply kissed her.

"I should like to purchase everything, please," I said. "Everything!"

Miss Alder laughed.

"That's what I expected," she said, "but I'm afraid you're a spendthrift, Lucinda."

She fetched my old tea-caddy and we counted out the sovereigns on the parlour table. "May I pay for the two hats now as well?" I asked.

"Certainly not," said Miss Alder. "Never pay for an article you've not seen."

"I should like Mamma to have a hat as well," I said.

173

"Is that a commission or merely a statement?" asked Miss Alder.

"Both," I cried and discovered, to my astonishment, that I was smiling.

That night, for the first time since I had come to live with Miss Alder, I dropped asleep without recollecting that Uncle Pescott hated me.

Chapter 29

FOURTEENTH BIRTHDAY

December 1857

I HAVE HAD A BIRTHDAY PARTY. IT WAS A SECRET ARRANGED between Miss Alder and Mamma. Mamma, with Flora and Isabella, George and little Harry, came to tea at Lion Cottage. I had been told that I was not to go to the Lodge that afternoon, but until Miss Alder began to lay the tea-table I had not guessed we were to have visitors.

When I saw Mamma and the others coming up the flagged path to the front door my joy was so great that my anxieties seemed to fly away.

Mamma brought me the painted fan and each of the others some home-made present. I was wearing the new merino dress that Miss Alder had given me. She gave me, too, a copy of *Pickwick Papers*. She is the kindest of friends.

The presents I had prepared were all wrapped in tissue paper and tied with coloured ribbons and we had placed them on the small table in the parlour.

After tea I distributed them. I was longing for Mamma to open the trinket package, but when she had unwrapped the locket and chain I saw how she suddenly covered her eyes and I knew that she was weeping.

I had never seen her weep before. Even when Papa died, she remained quiet and calm.

I felt tears start to my own eyes and I would have run to her, but Flora gave me a sharp pinch and slightly shook her head. So, for a few minutes, we all busied ourselves tidying the paper and ribbons and then Flora declared that a hat of Napoleon blue velvet was the one thing in the world that she had most longed for and we all trooped into the work-room so that she and Isabella could admire their new hats in Miss Alder's big mirror.

And by the time we returned to the parlour Mamma had fastened the locket round her neck and was helping Miss Alder to clear away the tea things.

Before she went home Mamma thanked me with a kiss and a few words that I shall never forget. But I shall not write them in my journal.

Chapter 30

LETTERS FROM MONTMARTRE

June 1858

I HAVE WRITTEN NOTHING IN MY JOURNAL FOR MONTHS. I HAVE been so engrossed in my poems and other things that the journal has seemed of little importance. I have also, of course, had to spend a good deal of each morning preparing my lessons for Mamma. But now I have to write a brief account of the events of the winter and spring.

We live so quietly that for me the most important events have been the letters I have received from Lot. He is still in France but not in Paris itself, since he has moved to a small country town, called Montmartre, at the gates of Paris. It is a town on a hill, with steep streets, no traffic and no policemen—a perfect place, I imagine, for anyone who wishes to sit down and paint in the open air. The shops are small and so are the houses, which are surrounded by leafy gardens. A number of artists live there and Lot seems very contented in his attic room where, from time to time, Miss Alder's cousin and her husband visit him. Lot moved from this kind lady's house in Paris because her daughter and son-in-law came on a long visit from Marseilles.

Lot's letters to me are gay and very short but he fills the margins and every space with tiny drawings of market-women and peasants, elegant ladies in enormous crinolines, and military gentlemen with great moustaches, small beards and the most wonderful helmets and busbies. It appears that every gentleman in Paris endeavours to look like the Emperor.

Lot writes more serious letters to Miss Alder. A picture-dealer is interested in his work and has sold a number of his paintings. "So," Lot said, "I can now eat—*and* buy all the paints and canvases I need." And he added, "My French has become so excellent that I can even purchase a loaf and six eggs without having either to point at them or draw them."

In another letter he wrote that he had seen the beautiful Eugénie, Empress of the French, driving in the Bois de Boulogne. "She is called 'La Reine Crinoline'," he said.

When Miss Alder read this to me a curious kind of disquiet crept into my mind. "I believe there are a great number of beautiful ladies in Paris," I said.

"No doubt there are some—as there are in most large cities," said Miss Alder. "And no doubt most ladies, young and not so young, aspire to be beautiful. But I've never heard that Paris has a monopoly of beautiful ladies."

"I'm glad of that," I said. "I don't wish Lot to find France *too* delightful. He was my friend and I miss him. In each letter we receive I hope he'll tell us that he's returning to Rindle Green. But sometimes I think he'll never come. I look at my picture first thing in the morning and last thing at night. And whenever I see the summer haze over the woods or the tree shadows in the grass I think, 'Lot would like that'. Even when the little children come to the Baby House to play I think, 'Lot should be here with his sketch-book'. But he never comes."

"Have you told him that you miss him?" asked Miss Alder.

"Of course not," I said. "He once said I was like a wasp and wasps don't miss people."

"If one is totally alone in the world, it may be pleasant to know that one is a little missed, even by a wasp," said Miss Alder.

"A little," I said. "I miss Lot a great deal. I miss him all the time—I believe I never stop missing him. We are so enclosed here in our valley that his letters seem our only window on the world. But when Lot himself was here I never felt we were shut away—I felt we were part of the world. Now I simply wait for him to come back."

The restoration of the Manor is almost complete, in spite of the fact that we had frost in March and snow in April. Now, this June evening, the weather is delightfully warm and our windows are wide open.

The small village gardens are full of larkspurs and roses, and the jasmine, that climbs round so many front doors, scents all the High Street at night.

I have not seen Uncle Pescott since All Saints' Day. Sometimes I catch a glimpse of his carriage as he drives through the village and once or twice I have stepped aside, into the baker's shop or down one of the small alleys, so that he would not be forced to see me.

The villagers watch him silently from between their curtains, and, if they should be in the street when his carriage passes, curtsy or touch their hats and then look away. They never smile or run out to call "Good Morning" as they do when Miss Alder walks down the High Street. I believe they all know, as I know now, that on the night of All Hallows Mamma defied Uncle Pescott. She insisted that if I were sent away to London, she and all the others would go too.

Uncle Pescott swore that if she went she would go without a penny from him and would receive no further assistance. If Miss Alder had not proposed that I should live at Lion Cottage we should have been not only penniless but without any kind of home.

It was Prue who told me what had occurred. That night she had hurried to the Lodge as soon as she heard I was missing. "I were makin' up the beds for Miss Flora and the others," she said. "I weren't listenin'. But the Squire were shoutin' so they could have heard him in Reyne and Ramsford. I don't hold with criticisin' the gentry but it wouldn't surprise me or Tom if the Squire had old Beezlebub's tail tucked up under his coat. You mark my words, Miss Luce—one day the Squire's goin' to——"

"I think Uncle Pescott can take care of himself, Prue," I said.

The villagers are very kind to me and I can scarcely step outside the gate but I am offered a nosegay of pinks or a few ripe strawberries on a leaf. Sometimes one of the old people, who can neither read nor write, knocks at our door with a letter from a daughter in London or a son in Birmingham and then, if Miss Alder is occupied in her work-room, I read the letter slowly aloud, several times, and usually write a reply. And the next day a couple of duck's eggs or a little fern in a pot will be left on the doorstep.

I believe the villagers are still talking of the fire at the Manor. So little happens in the country that it was an event of the most wonderful importance—of far greater interest than the rebuilding. I believe, too, that they pity me a little although I am in no need of pity, seeing that I have so courageous a Mamma and Miss Alder as a protector.

If only Lot would come back to Rindle Green—but I will not think of that.

Chapter 31

A CARRIAGE OUTSIDE
THE GATE

July 1858

A FORTNIGHT AGO, UNCLE PESCOTT CALLED AT LION COTTAGE. I can write this now without astonishment, but at the time I was quite astounded.

It was a warm evening and Miss Alder and I were sitting in the back garden, so we did not at first hear the knocking on the front door. But when at last I heard and ran to open the door, I found William, one of Uncle Pescott's footmen, on the doorstep. Uncle Pescott's carriage was waiting outside our front gate.

William grinned and wished me "Good evening."

I think I retreated into the passage too frightened to say a word, but William took a deep breath and announced that the Squire requested that Miss Alder would step outside for a moment and speak to him.

"I'll fetch Miss Alder," I said and wondered if I had unwittingly committed some new crime. I cannot see Uncle Pescott without expecting to be punished. Miss Alder put down her book and went out to the carriage.

She returned almost at once, a little flushed and, it seemed, more than a little vexed.

"Your Uncle merely wished to consult me about a choice of wallpaper for the school-room and bedrooms," she said. "I suggested that he should consult your Mother, who will have to see the papers every day. I fear I was not over-polite."

"Did Uncle Pescott mention me?" I asked, a little fearfully.

Miss Alder picked up her book.

"No," she said. "And when I told him what a pleasant companion you were, he appeared to grow suddenly deaf. I trust he will not call again on so small a pretext. I hoped he had come to—" but Miss Alder did not complete the sentence.

Uncle Pescott called again five days later, and it was Miss Alder who opened the door. William was again on the doorstep. I heard her say, "Pray tell the Squire that I've no wish to stand talking in the street," and William said, "Yes Miss," and was back in two minutes with the request that Miss Alder would "step up into the carriage to speak to the Squire."

"Pray tell the Squire that if he wishes to speak to me, it will be more comfortable in my parlour," said Miss Alder.

Apparently Uncle Pescott had no wish to descend from the carriage, and Miss Alder had already closed the front door when I heard the gate creak. Uncle Pescott was coming up the path. I began to tremble.

"I'll go to my room," I said, quickly.

"You'll do nothing of the sort," said Miss Alder. "Your family will soon be moving back into the Manor and you can't spend the next few years hiding away from your Uncle."

"But he said he never wanted to see me again," I said.

"Sit down," said Miss Alder, "and don't run away while I'm opening the door." So I sat down.

Uncle Pescott entered the parlour with his usual prancing step, and I hoped he would not observe me. He said, "Ah, Miss Alder! A beautiful evening! I see you have some fine roses in that bowl. We have some similar blooms in the Manor Garden, but I never recollect their name. I wish to speak to you in private."

"The rose is called 'Maiden's Blush'," said Miss Alder briskly, "and I think you can have nothing to say to me that Lucinda may not hear."

I dared not look at Uncle Pescott, but I hurriedly got to my feet and curtsied. Uncle Pescott appeared not to see me, and I sat down again.

"It is advisable to consult a lady of discrimination on household matters," said Uncle Pescott, "and I confess, too, that I am somewhat at a loss, Miss Alder, when I consider the numbers of new curtains, tablecloths and carpets which I shall be forced to purchase for the Manor. I need your expert advice, Miss Alder. But I must insist that this consultation of ours be in private."

"Insist?" said Miss Alder. And her voice was so sharp that it startled me. "I'd remind you, Mr. Pescott, that you are standing in my parlour and that Lucinda is my guest."

"Yes, yes," said Uncle Pescott. "But the matter can be of no interest—no possible interest—to any third party." He walked over to the window and spoke without looking at me. "Lucinda, there is no necessity for you to remain here."

I would thankfully have slipped away then, but Miss Alder said quietly, "Lucinda will stay where she is."

"I must ask you—" began Uncle Pescott, but Miss Alder gave him no time to finish.

"Your sister-in-law, Mr. Pescott, will doubtless provide you with all the assistance you need," she said. "Now, I beg you to excuse us as it is time for our supper."

"Indeed!" said Uncle Pescott. "But I had hoped—I'm persuaded, Miss Alder, that you are extremely well-informed in the matter of prices and the latest fashions in furnishings."

"I'm a village dressmaker," said Miss Alder. "Good evening, Mr. Pescott."

I imagined that after this visit, Uncle Pescott would not come near Lion Cottage again. But since then he has called four or five times. He has come in the afternoons, when I am at the

Lodge, and Miss Alder has told me little of these visits because, she says, there is little to tell.

"Your Uncle, I believe, comes here merely to talk of his plans and express his opinions," said Miss Alder. "Solitary people will talk to the most unresponsive listeners. Since I'm always busy, in my work-room, in the afternoons, I've given him little encouragement and, to tell you the truth, Lucinda, since Hallowe'en, I can scarcely endure his presence. If it were not for you and your family, I should make it quite clear that his visits are unwelcome."

The people of Rindle Green, of course, are deeply curious as to the meaning of Uncle Pescott's behaviour. I am aware of this, as one is always aware of things in a village—although only Prue has directly voiced her opinion. Nothing has ever prevented Prue from finding an explanation when she looked for one.

"You know what it is, Miss Luce," she said. "The Squire's been doin' a bit o' thinkin'. He aren't as young as he once were and I shouldn't wonder as you're sittin' on his conscience pretty heavy. You mark my words, Miss Luce—he's botherin' about that place down below, like the Rector tells us, where them little devils is busy throwin' red-hot coals about with their pitchforks and there aren't nothin' for miles and miles but fire and brimstone. The Squire don't want you hangin' like a millstone round his neck, Miss Luce, pullin' him down and down into all that nasty smoke and fire. He wants you back at the Manor with your Mamma. But he has to do it slow-like, because he aren't goin' to allow that he were ever wrong to send you away. So he come to see Miss Alder to slip in a word where it won't hardly be noticed."

Uncle Pescott has had a cold and has not been out of doors for a week. This morning, however, he sent a note to Miss Alder. "Would she drink a cup of tea with him in the library that afternoon?" He would send the carriage for her at four o'clock.

He had something of the greatest importance to discuss with her.

"I suppose your Uncle wishes to discuss footstools and fire irons this time," said Miss Alder. "The whole business has become ridiculous and I'm weary of it. He seems to believe that time is entirely at his disposal. It is *not*. And I shall send a refusal."

"Perhaps my Uncle wishes to tell you he'll see me again," I said.

"He's already seen you," said Miss Alder.

"He hasn't seen me, because, when he was here, he never once looked at me," I said. "I believe I care less than I did, but it's still dreadful to be so much hated. Sometimes I notice myself in the big mirror in the work-room and think, 'There I am! And Uncle Pescott never wants to set eyes on me again'. It makes me unhappy for hours afterwards. Fortunately I don't notice myself in the glass very often."

"So I've observed," said Miss Alder.

"Now the Manor is re-built, perhaps Uncle Pescott has begun to forgive me," I said. "Prue says——"

Miss Alder laughed. "The whole village knows what Prue is thinking," she said. "I suppose, one day, she may possibly be proved right. But it'll be a miracle."

"I should be very glad if you would go," I said. "Perhaps this *is* the miracle."

"Very well," said Miss Alder. "I'll go and drink tea in the library. And since, I suppose, your Mother will be there to pour it out, perhaps we can avoid the footstools and fire irons and talk about the crops and the weather—an infinitely more interesting subject."

Chapter 32

A CUP OF TEA IN THE LIBRARY

I WENT SO LATE TO BED LAST NIGHT AND WAS SO DISTURBED THAT I thought I should lie awake until daylight. But I dropped asleep at once. Now it is half past six, on a sweet fresh morning, and I shall write until breakfast-time.

Mamma, rather to my surprise, had tea with us as usual at the Lodge yesterday afternoon. I told her Miss Alder had been invited to the Manor and Mamma said she had not been informed. She seemed to grow a little pale and I observed that she had difficulty in giving her full attention to our questions during the lessons. She has been so well and cheerful lately that her uneasiness distressed me.

Miss Alder called for me at half past five, far earlier than I had expected. She had walked down the drive. She went straight to Mamma and took her hand.

"There's no need for anxiety, my dear," she said. "The Squire is not contemplating any kind of change." Then she turned to me and said we must be getting back to Rindle Green.

"But surely the carriage should be here?" I said.

"I informed the Squire that I preferred to walk," said Miss Alder.

"I've been told nothing, absolutely nothing," said Mamma. "But I believe we've great cause to thank you."

"The facts are not worth the telling," said Miss Alder. "And

186

thanks, between friends, are unnecessary. Come, Lucinda!"
She kissed Mamma with a kind of brisk tenderness and we
hurried away. We had almost reached the half-way tree before
she spoke again.

"I scarcely know," she said, "whether I'm most angry with
myself, the Squire or this stupid world, which allows women so
little say in its affairs and permits small-minded men to become
despots. I believed that I had lived long enough for nothing to
surprise me and yet, this afternoon, I was so astonished and
taken aback that my wits almost deserted me. I shall not see the
Squire again."

"Did he make any mention of me?" I asked timidly.

"He spoke, at great length, entirely of himself, his hopes and
his plans," said Miss Alder.

After supper, I slipped out to the front gate to make sure that
I had fastened it. Occasionally one of the village dogs pushes
through into the front garden and breaks the stocks and snap-
dragons. There were a crowd of villagers standing outside our
gate, talking together and, it seemed, arguing in considerable
excitement, And even as I approached, others joined them. I
heard one of the women say. "That Prue's a liar and always has
been," and another answered, "Eh, now—she's a good girl and
means no harm. It's just that her tongue runs away with her."

"Well, it's run too far this time," said the first woman. "The
Squire aren't likely to put up with such a wicked bit o' tarradid-
dlin'. There's not a soul in the village but have heard it by now
and the Squire himself'll hear it before mornin'."

"Let him hear it," said another woman. "Our Prue's worth
ten o' the Squire."

They were all so engrossed in their conversation that they
did not notice me until I fastened the gate and it gave its usual
squeak. Then there was a sudden silence.

"Ask Miss Luce," said somebody.

"For shame! How should she know?" said one of the men.

"No need to ask," said the first woman. "Truth's truth. And

if an angel came down out o' the sky, I'd still say Prue's a liar."

"I don't know what you're talking about," I said, "but Prue does *not* tell lies. She has a great deal of imagination, that's all. Where is Prue?"

"She went indoors," said the second woman. "It's a cruel shame—the things some has been sayin' about her."

"I believe it would be a good thing if we all went indoors," I said. "In the morning, I'm sure Prue will be able to explain—"

"Yes, Miss Luce," they said. But nobody moved.

"Lies is lies," said the first woman, "and there aren't no sense in calling them different. Lies is lies, and always will be."

I went slowly back to the cottage. It was almost half past eight. I should have asked Miss Alder to go out and speak to them, but she had gone to her room immediately after supper, with a bad headache. Later, when I looked out, it seemed that at least half the village had gathered silently outside our gate in the High Street. They were staring at our front door as though waiting for Miss Alder to appear. But I had no wish to disturb her. I locked the doors for the night and went up to my room.

I was brushing my hair, when I heard a knocking at the back door, and put down my brush and hurried downstairs with my candle. Prue stood outside and with her were her father and Tom. They had walked up the garden from the alley at the back, to avoid the crowd.

Prue said, "Oh, Miss Luce—Oh, please Miss Luce—" and then to my consternation, burst into tears.

"Come in," I said. "All of you." And I quickly closed the door.

"We've come to see Miss Alder," said Mr. Pryor. "It's late, Miss Luce, but the matter can't be held over till the mornin'. My girl's been called a liar and she never been that. And only Miss Alder or the Squire can say as she aren't."

"Miss Alder had a headache," I said, "and I hope she's gone to bed. But come into the parlour."

Prue's eyes were swollen and red with weeping and she

188

looked at me piteously. "They'd listen to you, Miss Luce, if you'd say to them it were true," she said.

"But I'm quite in the dark, Prue," I said. "I was having my lessons at the Lodge when Miss Alder called on Uncle Pescott this afternoon."

"And haven't Miss Alder said a word?" asked Tom, and I noticed he was holding Prue's hand in a very kind and protective manner.

"Miss Alder's told me nothing," I said, "but she doesn't wish to see Uncle Pescott again."

"And doesn't that prove it?" said Prue. "It's as true as I stands here. I hear it all, word for word. I were rubbin' a bit o' polish on the floor outside o' the library and the Squire begins shoutin'. Miss Alder must have spoke more quiet, in between, but the Squire weren't listenin'. He went on and on. And it's true what I said, Miss Luce. I never been a liar, never! You tell them, that's outside."

"But, Prue, I don't know what you did say," I said. "And I can't wake Miss Alder now."

"But they called my girl a liar and the mornin's too late for settin' *that* right," said Mr. Pryor. Prue wiped her eyes with the hand that Tom was not holding.

"I hear the Squire call out that he knew no lady like bein' named an old maid," said Prue. "Then he shout that it were right and proper to take one's time but he weren't one to wait for ever. Then he says that everythin' were easy enough to arrange. Your Mamma would be given eighty pounds a year in London, and Miss Flora and Miss Isabella was old enough to go out as governesses. Miss Alder must ha' said somethin' then, because the Squire shout that didn't she understand that he were offerin' her to be mistress of the Manor? And that weren't no small honour for a village dressmaker.

"Quite soon after that the door were opened and Miss Alder come out o' the library and hurried to the front door and never see me at all. So I gets up off my knees and goes after her to open the door. But she were already flyin' down the drive. And I couldn't hardly believe what I hear, Miss Luce, but it were all true."

A feeling of dreadful helplessness and misery had taken hold of me and I discovered I was gripping the edge of the table. Uncle Pescott, after all, had been planning to send Mamma and the others away. Mamma had defied him, on the night of the fire and this was his answer. And I was responsible because I had started the fire. (I had entirely forgotten Miss Alder's kind words to Mamma.)

"You *has* to believe me, Miss Luce," said Prue, and I said, "Yes, Prue, I do."

Then I thought I should offer them each a cup of tea and begged them to sit down.

"I must make up the kitchen fire," I said, "and put the kettle on." And then the parlour door opened and Miss Alder came in. She said, "I thought I heard voices. Sit down, all of you. What is it, Prue?" She was fully dressed but I could see that her headache still troubled her.

"Some of them outside is saying I'm a liar," said Prue. "Tell them, Miss, that it were true what I hear this afternoon."

"Were you listening?" asked Miss Alder sharply.

"I were polishin'," said Prue, "and the Squire begin shoutin'—"

"I see," said Miss Alder, "and I suppose, by now, the whole village knows what you heard the Squire shouting?"

"I only tell what I hear when I were polishin'," said Prue. "But they're sayin' I'm a liar. They're sayin' the Squire would never——"

"Yes," said Miss Alder. "I can understand they find it difficult to believe. I was, myself, astonished. But you shouldn't polish outside a closed door, Prue, when the Squire's engaged in conversation on the other side of it. You see that it can lead to all kinds of difficulties."

"Yes, Miss," said Prue. "But will you tell them——"

"I had hoped the whole matter was closed and that no one, apart from the Squire and myself, knew of it," said Miss Alder, slowly.

"Yes, Miss," said Prue. "but will you tell them——"

"Prue weren't never a liar," said Tom, "but there's some as says she is. A word like that sticks, Miss, and the village won't never forget it. Is it so much to ask, Miss, that you should tell them Prue were right?"

"Yes," said Miss Alder. "It's a very great deal to ask. I'd given my word. And others, beside myself, are indirectly involved. However—" she stood up. "It's time we were all in bed," she said. She stepped into the passage, opened the front door and walked down the path to the gate.

Prue, Tom and Mr. Pryor followed her, but I, not knowing what I should do, hesitated in the open doorway. A nearly full moon was shining and our front garden was bright with moon-light. Miss Alder stopped by the gate and spoke so clearly that I could hear every word.

"Prue told the exact truth," she said. "This afternoon the Squire made me a proposal of marriage and I refused. Now go home, all of you. Goodnight."

She turned and walked back up the path. "Lock the doors, Lucinda," she said. "I don't know what Prue told you, but I'll see that no harm comes to your family."

Chapter 33

UNCLE PESCOTT DRIVES AWAY

WE BREAKFASTED LATE THIS MORNING. MISS ALDER ADMITTED that she had slept little during the night, so I carried a chair into the garden for her and told her I would wash the breakfast things and dust the parlour. I hoped she would rest but she had, she said, a letter to write.

"This morning, I'm at home to nobody," she said.

I was peeling the potatoes when I heard a hammering on the front door and flew to open it and send away the unwelcome visitor. But I had scarcely unlocked the door when Uncle Pescott pushed past me into the passage.

"I wish to speak to Miss Alder," he said.

"Miss Alder is not at home," I said, but he thrust me ahead of him into the passage and demanded to know where Miss Alder was.

"She's quite worn out and not at home to anyone," I said. "Pray go away, Uncle Pescott."

"Very fine!" said Uncle Pescott. "Very fine indeed! I am not surprised to hear that Miss Alder is fatigued. She must have been talking half the night."

I believe I glanced apprehensively at the back door, fearing that Miss Alder might hear his raised voice. And Uncle Pescott must have observed me. He let go my shoulder and before I could prevent him, strode down the passage, flung open the back door and rushed into the garden.

I heard a startled exclamation from Miss Alder and then Uncle Pescott's loud, angry voice, and I hurried after him, with the desperate and foolish intention of trying to protect Miss Alder from his wrath.

But she appeared to be in no need of my assistance. She was sitting in her chair with the letter, which she had already addressed, on the garden table beside her, waiting in silence until Uncle Pescott should stop.

His rage had taken such complete possession of him that he had begun to shout and I thought, thankfully, that there were no little children playing in the Baby House or in the alley at the end of the garden. They would have heard every word. When, at last, Uncle Pescott paused for breath, Miss Alder stood up.

"Now, perhaps, you'll be good enough to listen to me, Mr. Pescott," she said, in her usual matter-of-fact voice. "Yesterday, you made me a proposal of marriage, but it was quite clear that all you wished for was an unpaid housekeeper to take the place of your sister-in-law. You announced that you believed me to be a capable and economical woman and stressed the fact that, since I had a small fortune of my own, we should be unlikely to disagree over money matters. And you added that since I was without relatives, and must now be reckoned an old maid, you believed I would receive your suggestion with pleasure. Pleasure, Mr. Pescott! I received your proposal with the utmost displeasure."

Uncle Pescott would have spoken then, but Miss Alder continued.

"You will allow me to finish what I have to say. You have broken in on my privacy and dared to upbraid me for making the matter public. I must tell you that I said nothing whatever about our interview until I discovered that the entire village knew the story.

"You alone, Mr. Pescott, are to blame. You raised your voice in the library yesterday as you have raised it this morning in my garden, and you were overheard. If you wish your affairs to remain private, you should learn to modulate your voice."

She picked up the letter. "When you so rudely invaded my garden, Mr. Pescott, I had just finished writing to you, to tell you that the whole business had become public knowledge and that any attempt at secrecy would be both useless and ridiculous. Here is the letter."

Uncle Pescott took the letter and thrust it into his pocket.

"You should have denied everything," he said. "Everything! You gave me to understand that the affair would be totally forgotten if I allowed my sister-in-law and the children to remain at the Manor. You should have denied—"

I saw Miss Alder frown.

"Our strict rules of politeness and decorum do not always lead to perfect honesty," she said, "but I've never lied, Mr. Pescott, on the grand scale that you suggest. I might, of course, have remained silent. But I confirmed the story because otherwise a good-hearted girl would have been branded as a liar."

"And in saving the skin of some miserable village girl, you were prepared to make me a laughing-stock," cried Uncle Pescott. "Or perhaps that did not occur to you?"

"It occurred to me but did not seem of great importance," said Miss Alder.

Uncle Pescott began to stamp up and down Miss Alder's small plot of grass. "A laughing-stock!" he cried. "A laughing-stock in Rindle Green today and in Rindlebridge and Reyne tomorrow! I know these village gossips! And in two days' time, Ramsford itself and most of the County will have heard the story. The Squire of Rindle Green is too well-known, too much a personage to be spared. Tongues will wag and the news will fly along every lane and byway, of how the Squire of Rindle Green was refused by the village dressmaker. And every time I walk into church or drive out in the carriage there will be

195

sly glances and half-smiles and whispers. The story may even reach the ears of the Honourable Mrs. Billing."

And Uncle Pescott seemed almost to groan as he trampled the neatly cut grass.

"You make too much of the matter," said Miss Alder, sharply. "You're not the only man to have been refused nor am I the only woman to prefer spinsterhood."

"Too much!" cried Uncle Pescott. "Too much!" He stood still and began to dig small holes in the turf with his stick. "I have always despised these stupid villagers," he said. "Their minds are as impoverished as their cottages. For Rindle Green, every trifling happening has the importance of a national event. It is discussed for years and never forgotten. What then must I expect? What endure? In London, the lower orders do, at least, possess a certain life of their own and quickness of mind but here, in the country——"

"Here, in the country, I shall be grateful if you'll respect my grass," said Miss Alder.

"Here, where the general dullness is only lightened by stupid out-worn festivals and endless gossip, my existence will be insupportable," cried Uncle Pescott. "I shall be an object of ridicule to every Tom, Dick and Harry."

(Suddenly I was reminded of the snail Uncle Pescott had talked of in the library. He had said, "A man without money is like a snail without a shell and is at the mercy of every Tom, Dick and Harry who may choose to trample over him. A man with money is armed against the world.")

But it seemed that money proved but poor armour.

"I have always revered my forbears," said Uncle Pescott, "and the huge sums I have spent on the Manor bear witness to that veneration. I have spared neither time nor thought—indeed I may say that I have thought of little else since I inherited the property. Yet I would abandon my life here, my position and all the authority I have gained to escape from the situation in which you, Madam, have placed me. I would even sell the

Manor itself, the estate, everything—if I could. Unfortunately it is entailed. It must remain in the family and be passed on to my brother's children."

"I see no reason why *you* should stay here," said Miss Alder quickly. "Go back to London. You have, I believe, a house there. London is very large and I doubt if one Londoner in five thousand has ever heard of Rindle Green. You will be known only as a man of means, with property in the country."

There was a sudden silence. Then Uncle Pescott began to shout again.

"Very fine! Very fine indeed! And for whose sake, pray, am I to remove myself? For your sake or my own? You take a great deal on yourself, Madam, when you suggest that I shall leave the Manor. Am I to presume that my presence, a mile away, is likely to cause you so much uneasiness that——"

"You may assume what you choose," said Miss Alder, "but I was thinking neither of you nor of myself. I was thinking of your sister-in-law and the children. You have transformed the Manor, that should have been a home, into a monument and forgotten that you live in a world peopled by human creatures who exist in their own right and were not created merely to be exploited."

"One must either exploit or be exploited," said Uncle Pescott. "I learned that years ago when I worked in the City. There was another clerk in the office, younger than I, a stupid, tall fellow without an iota of my quickness or capability. He came and went as he pleased, but I worked—sometimes until nearly midnight. Yet it was he who became the junior partner because his Grandpapa left him a thousand pounds and he placed it at the firm's disposal. One is a fool if one refuses to learn from experience."

"One is, perhaps, an even greater fool if one permits a single experience to poison one's life," said Miss Alder.

The clock in the passage struck faintly and I counted the strokes. It was eleven o'clock.

"Doubtless it was Prudence Pryor who listened yesterday at the library door," said Uncle Pescott. "She shall be sent packing at once and will get neither wages nor a reference from me."

"That will not greatly disturb her. I believe she intends to marry at Michaelmas," said Miss Alder.

"As to my return to London," said Uncle Pescott, "it is impossible. The affairs of the Manor and the farm and the entire estate force me to remain here. I have never been able to discover an honest factotum and the whole property would disintegrate without my constant labours." And he began to pace up and down again.

"I've been told," said Miss Alder briskly, "that I'm both a capable and an economical manager. I'll be your factotum, Mr. Pescott. And you may leave for London tomorrow."

Uncle Pescott stood still and stared at her with an expression of such astonishment that, had I been less astonished myself, I believe I should have laughed.

"I've grown a little weary of concocting costumes for ladies who have so little to do that they find it necessary to change their dresses seven times a day," said Miss Alder. "I've no intention of closing my establishment in London, but I myself shall in future make dresses only for my friends. So I shall have time on my hands and am willing to sit in your library, Mr. Pescott, for six mornings a week, and supervise everyone and everything." And she added, "For the sum of fifty-two pounds a year."

There was another silence and this time it lasted longer. "It is a pity—a great pity—that you belong to the gentler sex," said Uncle Pescott after the pause. "Fifty-two pounds is reasonable enough and had you been a man I believe I should—but no, it would never do! No woman is fitted to do a man's work. No woman has the farsightedness, the quickness of mind or the authority. No woman has the grasp of essentials or the knowledge—in short, it would *not* do. Good morning!"

"Good morning!" said Miss Alder. "Will you see your Uncle to the door, Lucinda."

A small crowd had gathered round the carriage outside our gate and, as Uncle Pescott stepped down the path an old man shouted, "Been 'avin' another try, Squire?"

"She won't have him—how so ever often he tries," cried a woman, and another answered, "Small blame to her."

Uncle Pescott stopped as though he had been struck by a stone. Then he turned and walked back into the cottage, and I followed quickly.

"Tell the carriage to wait in the back alley," said Uncle Pescott and hurried down the passage into the garden again.

I heard him say, "My situation is intolerable. I *cannot* remain here. I shall agree to anything you propose."

It was past eight o'clock now and Prue has just gone. She was a little pale but quite cheerful. "The Squire come home with a face like a black earthquake," she said, "and sent me off without a bit o' notice or wages. But Tom say it don't matter. It seems the Squire's off to London and the Manor's like a ant-heap that's been trod on. The Squire's rushin' round with a bit o' chalk markin' all them things that's to be took to London. All them big pictures is to go and so's the dolls' house. Maybe the Squire's goin' to show it to the Prince o' Wales and all his little brothers and sisters. You mark my words, Miss Luce—the Squire aren't comin' back to Rindle Green in a hurry."

"I believe he's not coming back at all, Prue," I said.

Chapter 34

FIFTEENTH BIRTHDAY:
THE MANOR

December 1858

TODAY, DECEMBER 4TH, 1858, IS MY FIFTEENTH BIRTHDAY AND Mamma gave me, as usual, the painted fan. But as we are now no longer penniless I also received from her a delightful small clock for my green bedroom.

Indeed, I have had such a number of presents that I feel extraordinarily rich.

Only Lot forgot my birthday.

Months ago he asked me, in one of his letters, when my birthday was, and now he has not sent me a single word. If the weather were not so still and mild I would tell myself that Lot's letter had been held up by a storm at sea.

I have not opened my journal since Uncle Pescott found it expedient to return to London. He left without farewells, writes to no one and only briefly acknowledges Miss Alder's monthly reports. But he pays Mamma two hundred pounds a year and we live at the Manor as we would in our own home. And I grow ever fonder of the great rooms and the sweet views from the windows.

Even the dark winter has no terror now. When the weather is cold we have fires in our bedrooms, the water in our jugs no longer freezes and the rooms are lighted at night by clear-burning lamps.

And the school-room chimney, since it was re-built, no longer smokes.

I have now a room of my own. The green bedroom was untouched by the fire so I can still admire the flowers on the old wallpaper and can sit, if I wish, like an Arab in his tent, behind the bed curtains. But the curtains are new and I have now no need to wrap myself in a dust sheet for warmth when I wish to write.

Often I discover that I am staring at the spot, near the window, where Lot used to sit when he was painting the dolls' house pictures. That was only a year and a half ago, yet so much has happened since then that it seems like twenty years. Perhaps I should no longer recognise Lot—or perhaps he would see me as some unknown young lady. It is sad to grow old.

There is a faint mist today and it occurs to me that there may be fog in the Channel. Perhaps that is why Lot's letter has not come.

When we moved back to the Manor Flora and Isabella still wished to share a bedroom. It seems that Flora can never express her sentiments and her hopes often enough to satisfy Isabella and they hold long conversations far into the night. I know this only because George and Harry share the bedroom next door to them and George complains that the murmur of their voices keeps him awake.

George and Harry now ride, each morning, to the Grammar School at Ramsford, and Tom rides with them as far as Rindle-bridge, where they join the red-haired son of the Rector. As he teaches at the school he completes the journey with them and rides back to the Rectory with them in the afternoon. Tom fetches them from the Rectory. Miss Alder quietly arranged this. The boys are delighted to have their lessons with other boys and even more delighted to possess ponies of their own.

Flora, Isabella and I continue our lessons with Mamma, but

twice a week we are driven to Ramsford for French and piano-forte lessons. I enjoy the French lessons.

If Lot ever comes home I intend to greet him in perfect French.

The mist is clearing a little, so perhaps there will be a letter soon. As for the son of the Rector of Rindlebridge—he is our most frequent visitor at week-ends and in the holidays. His name is James and he rides up, on his piebald horse, with jam from his mother or embroidery patterns from his sister or books from his father. He joins us in whatever we happen to be doing, talks with everyone but Flora and usually rides away within the hour. But his eyes stray always in Flora's direction and Flora herself seems to shine with such beauty when he is here—and is so sweetly amiable after his visits—that I believe it will not be long before he asks Mamma's permission and becomes a member of our family.

I am writing this in the library where dear Miss Alder is dealing with all the business of the day. It pleases me to hear her ordering the affairs of the estate, and she works with such calmness, such knowledge and such good humour that no one has ever questioned her authority. Sometimes it has seemed to me that she knows more about the rotation of crops, the drainage and manuring of fields and the thinning of woodlands than the country people themselves.

When I asked her how she had learnt so much she smiled. "When I decided to live in Rindle Green, I set myself the task of becoming a countrywoman," she said. "I listened to village talk, asked questions and read all I could about the cultivation of land. You must remember, too, that for years I drove about the countryside, from house to house, and saw other fields and woods than those in the Rindle Valley, and other estates. When I was weary of Fashion and even more weary of fashionable women it was a relief to turn to the contemplation of barley and oats."

Often Miss Alder and Mamma confer together and, listening

to their quiet voices, I marvel at the way in which the library has changed. Yet the actual differences between what it was and what it is are few. The walls, that were once covered with great paintings, are bare and the dolls' house has gone.

Miss Alder sits at Uncle Pescott's desk and, next to my green bedroom, the library is now the room I love best in the Manor.

The village has changed too. Roofs that had leaked for years have been repaired and rotting floorboards and window frames have been renewed. Miss Alder inspected each one of Uncle Pescott's cottages in Rindle Green and ordered all that was necessary. Several of the villagers protested that they were well enough off as they were, but most of them were thankful that they had no longer to put buckets to catch the drips when it rained or walk warily on their upper floors.

Mrs. Marden's cottage was her own and there was no one to inherit it but Sophie's husband. Miss Alder succeeded in tracing him, but he had no wish to own a half-ruined cottage in Rindle Green. So, with Miss Alder's assistance, I have bought it for Mamma with my seventy-one gold sovereigns that remained. A lawyer in Ramsford arranged the transaction and Mamma will let it. Tom and Mr. Pryor have been renovating it, in their spare time, and Tom and Prue, who are now married, will move into it as soon as it is re-painted. I believe Prue scrubs it, from top to bottom, at least once a week. She has come back to the Manor.

"I has to keep an eye on you, Miss Luce," she said, "and your Mamma can still do with a bit o' fussin' after. And I don't want no wages."

So Miss Alder has simply raised Tom's wages by ten shillings a week.

I was very glad when Prue returned. "Since the Squire aren't the Squire no longer," she said, "it's like that garden the Rector tells us about, Miss Luce—the garden where that Eve pick the apple and the snake come down out o' the apple tree."

"You mean the Garden of Eden," I said.

"Yes, that's right," said Prue. "Only now there aren't no snake."

Miss Alder always has her mid-day meal with us and immediately afterwards Tom harnesses Thimble and she drives back to the village.

I have just waved her "goodbye" as I always do. It is still a little misty, but the sun is struggling to appear. I hope there is no fog now over the sea. Miss Alder has made me promise to walk up to my beech-tree chair this afternoon. "You seem a little melancholy, Lucinda," she said, "and the exercise will do you good. I should like to see you with rosy cheeks when I return for your birthday tea."

"I'll do my best," I said.

So now I am about to put on my old bonnet and take my walk.

As I climbed High Meadow the sun showed for an instant like a silver ghost, and then lost itself again in the mist. The path through the woods smelt of fallen leaves and decay, and the soft air and half-seen trees seemed part of so universal a sorrow that my melancholy deepened into a kind of pain. I had lived for fifteen years, my childhood was done and Lot had not remembered to write to me.

My armchair was full of dead leaves. I brushed them away, spread several sheets of newspaper and sat down.

(We subscribe to a newspaper now, because Mamma believes that we should take an interest in the affairs of the world.)

The mist in the valley was thinning. Already the far hills and dark stretches of woodland were emerging and I could clearly see the curve of the river.

The Manor stood like a giant's dolls' house on its slope, and the restoration was so complete that no one, looking down on it from the woods, would have guessed that fire had so recently swept through half the rooms.

In the afternoon stillness I could hear Harry calling to George in the orchard and the faint clatter of the pump in the stable yard. I began to compose a poem to Autumn.

Then, suddenly, there was a rustling in the hazel bushes behind me and a man came quickly down my root stairs and stood still, a little below me staring at the valley. I could see nothing of him but his back and that had a slightly foreign appearance. But my heart began to beat and I hurriedly stood up.

The man turned and his hand went up to his head as though he would have raised his hat. But he had no hat.

"Good afternoon," he said.

"Good afternoon," I said. And a wave of joy swept all my melancholy away.

"Am I trespassing?" he asked.

"No, oh, no," I cried. "The prospect of the valley is extremely beautiful from here, isn't it?"

"That should have been my remark," said Lot.

"I didn't expect you," I said. "If I'd known you were coming I'd have prepared a welcome in perfect French. Our phrase-book is a little old-fashioned but I can ask you, in French, what o'clock it is or tell you that I love milk, butter and cheese or call your attention to the Steeples of Dover."

Lot looked up at me and laughed and I was filled with contentment.

"Are you going to stay—" I began and then changed the question and asked if the ladies in France were very beautiful.

"I've heard they're excessively beautiful," said Lot, "but they wear crinolines of such enormous size that no one can approach them. One needs opera glasses before one can admire their features. And I've no opera glasses. Weren't you going to ask me another question?"

"Yes," I said. "Have you brought much luggage with you?"

"I've brought all the paintings I didn't sell. And my paints and brushes," said Lot. "What other luggage did you expect me to bring?"

"I don't know," I said. "Have you made any plans?"

"Are you asking me if I'm going to remain here?" asked Lot.

"Yes," I said. "Only I was afraid—"

"I'm going to paint the Rindle Valley," said Lot. "And I've already settled into my old room in the Baby House. I've spent the morning arranging an exhibition in Miss Alder's workroom and now you're to walk back with me and choose a picture for your birthday. Your Mamma has already given her permission. And I've been invited to your birthday tea-party. *Mes félicitations cordiales, Mademoiselle*, on your fifteenth anniversary. And if ever I return to France——"

"Oh, Lot," I said, "*please, please* don't speak of it—not now, not on my birthday."

"I notice you're wearing only a very small crinoline," said Lot, "and that's extremely fortunate because, if ever I return to France, I shall be able to pack you into my carpet bag, with my brushes and paints (and, of course, your Mamma's permission) and take you with me. But you'll have to promise never to look over your shoulder. I'll guarantee to feed you on milk, butter and cheese and you'll be able to spend your days asking what o'clock it is because I've still no watch and never know the time. As to the Steeples of Dover—you're not crying, are you Lucinda?"

"No," I said, "I'm not," and I shut my eyes quickly while two tears, of pure happiness, slipped down my cheek.

When I opened my eyes the sun had come out. The Rindle Valley seemed to stretch to the ends of the earth. And it was filled with light.